My Difficult Man

My Difficult Man

Disha Ganguly

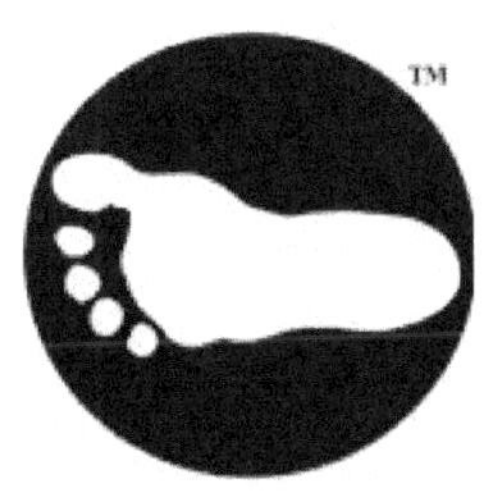

Bigfoot Publications

Because, there's a writer in everyone.

My Difficult Man
Author : Disha Ganguly

First Published by
Bigfoot06 Publications (OPC) Pvt. Ltd. B-10,12
Shree Shyam Palace,
Sector 4,5 Chowk, Old Railway Road,
Gurugram, Haryana (122001)
Website: www.bigfootpublications.in
Email: info@bigfootpublications.in

First Edition: January 2023
©Disha Ganguly

ISBN Print Book - 978-93-90925-97-1

Printed in India

Just felt like saying,

To all the girls who are struggling, losing, breaking down into pieces, but showing up again the next day, Your stories are heard, noted and valued.

You are never alone.

ACKNOWLEDGEMENT

This novel has become possible all the way because of my parents, my two best friends – Arijit and Sneha Bansal and my darling flatmate Riya.

INDEX

1. Ceasefire Of Senses _________________________ 1

2. My Delicious Stranger _______________________ 12

3. The Lost Call _____________________________ 25

4. The Friendly Invitation ______________________ 44

5. Our Magic ________________________________ 59

6. L'Amour __________________________________ 73

7. The Sun And The Storm ______________________ 80

8. My Note __________________________________ 92

9. Adventure Next Door ________________________ 106

10. Spurt Of Hope ____________________________ 118

11. The Monsoon Worth Waiting For ______________ 135

12. Kanishk & Life ___________________________ 143

13. The Meltdown Begins _______________________ 154

14. Season 'Me' ______________________________ 169

15. How Human Are You, Kanishk? ________________ 181

16. "Run" ___________________________________ 190

17. Words Of The Devil ________________________ 212

CEASEFIRE OF SENSES

Vandalism seems wittier, to be watched from a distance. But when it snatches away the textbook ground of your life, it's probably the worst obituary you ever wish to write. I would probably be a preacher of a silent death dome, or a new face of third world comedy for the first world people, or a hermit away from home and childhood naiveté, or a novice detective crippling inside the web of tenures, or making a big buffet breakfast with rolls and corn dogs for my family, but no! The universe chose me to throw into some voyage, where at the edge of the largest wave, he was waiting for me. On the way of my less and pale life, he came with a pint of colors and took it back with him. Once in a while, in the middle of a starry night, he took me away to be a part of his fairy tale, a tale that tells the enchantment of the hidden world of shadows.

My stumpy story engraved its root in an adolescent winter, just like some other teeny kid. But when I reached its climax, neither was it adolescent, nor was I a naïve teen. It made me break all the barriers of possibilities, and when I think back, I realize that the commencement did me with no caution.

Winters are more adorable when you have a seat just beside your date, crossing fingers without any rut, bringing the spring upon your fingertips. Even when you're not bothered to be bothered about how hard puberty is hitting and how to channelize your mainstream ongoings in a fruitful way, then it's your time to be a witness of a sudden fall. Teenage is all about the ardor.

Going to a coffee shop with the tuition bag, as if your mom knows that you are at tuition, struggling a lot to make a strong seat among ten lakhs of boards' students, even when your brother is an IIT topper and hopes hard to see you as successful as he is, but the inner-self has already reckoned that you are a big dud for good grades and can't even envision IIT in day-mares, life is hard for you. But here, my mind is objectifying smugness inside my date, nudging me into pheromones and keeping me warm with the thoughts of being together. Staring at our intimate fingers by leaning on his shoulder, somehow my feisty soul is dying a slow death. This palpable dominance is amusing. For moments, he is that perfect I always wanted.

Ishaan is boasting about his love for his camera and how amazing features it has (with a price which can bring me two new scooters together). His jibber jabber is not just only strangling out my brain but also amplifying my dumbness to let him bring his camera on our date. It was supposed to be romantic as I expected him to click some good pictures of us. But I think I was probably wrong. He has a very minimal sense of romanticism and when the other person is me, it's not very easy to pretend the idea of love I want from him.

I am never against of the people with expensive passions but I never possibly respect those who lay on exaggerating their capabilities for gaining some fake validations. I am not in the mood of slogging his lectures off on our date, so I behave well suppressing my resentful expressions that were ready to blast out. At least I don't want to let him make a bizarre impression on me after burning my pocket for the stupid foods he ordered and ate the most of it.

I can't say that I was much into the afterglow of the date; but spending time with Ishaan isn't that suffocating. When we started seeing each other as something more than friends, going out with him was more like bringing an adrenaline rush every time. I used to eagerly wait for weekends, so that I could go out with him and escape the entangled burden of school syllabus for a bit. But as the time started proceeding, I couldn't find any plausible explanation of losing the spark between us. Though I am still ready to rejuvenate the old feelings for him, it doesn't seem the same from the other end. Sometimes I can't trust my downward desires for the opposite gender. This age is brutal.

Ishaan and I have been dating for a year now. He came to my neighborhood when I was urging fourteen and he was a charming lad of sixteen. His house is just a yard apart. Though mine looks very pale and unappealing in comparison with his Richie-rich high-class architecture, I never heard him boasting over it. His mom is a very kind-hearted lady with some impressive social skills and as usual, it didn't take enough time for our parents to become very close friends. His father is a rich businessman who never travels other than business class, and does party with the elite society people whom we probably call untouchables. According to his dad, his mom was never a good fit in his life, so he better prefers staying in different cities, away from his former wife and son.

We used to go to the same school, and there we became friends. Somehow his mom's good influence never let his dad sow the sky-kissing pride in him. I met his dad hardly twice in all these years, and never felt any good in him that should reflect from his behavior. Kanishk, my elder brother, got to know about Ishaan for a few months before he left for IIT Bombay for his engineering. Nikhil, my best friend from the very first day I got to know the meaning of the word 'Friend', also had good bro-ship with him. But in these growing years, I gradually grew some feelings for him, and last December in the middle of a COD match, he confessed that not all the time he opened his window to see the greenery of the yard; some openings were for me too, to keep checking in. Nikhil was there to destroy my self-respect by readily confirming that I also had the same thoughts for him. From then, we were more than friends, less than lovers.

I use the term '*more than friends, less than lovers*' cause there were no official *ILoveYou* kind of proposals. He said he liked me a lot and he wanted to explore this feeling for further connection. In this age, this confusion between love and lust is normal, especially when the person is never getting out of your sight. We went to a lot of dates, but every day ended up with a dumb conversation. As we know everything about each other, we often run out of topics. But the thing that I never want to change about this relationship or the situationship whatever it's called, is the bonding. I had a crush on him since the day we made a Go-As-You-Like competition together. I was the Tinker bell to his Peter Pan and none of our cool-school-kids thought to be this much creative to get the first place. Our principal declared that we looked '*really good*' together and the butterflies in my stomach started going round and round imagining him as the sexiest boyfriend I can get at this age. A lot of girls at our school had a crush on him, even some of them were older, as he was a popular boy and mostly a ladies' boy for some very valid reasons. He was handsome, played good guitar tunes, and basketball, had four-pack abs with a sexy smirk. So, having him as a date was supposed to be true only in my dreams.

Reaching home, I throw my shoes off and stride towards my room as if I am too tired with exams and doubt clearing sessions for three long hours. These days are so colorful that the burden of lies doesn't have any effect on me anyway. But when the thoughts of my upcoming exam slither into my vision, I feel like a voyeur of my own career.

"Kichu Khabe?" (Want something to eat?)

"Sure"

"Wash yourself and come to the table."

"Yeah"- And I enter into my room keeping the door closed. After settling my bag in the book rack, I saw Ishaan was putting off his clothes to the bed and his four-pack ab was glittering in sweat. I wasn't trying to sneak into his room, but who would like to miss the chance to see Ishaan Khandelwal shirtless. Maybe this is the reason we are missing out the spark, to be seen by each other every time, every day whenever we want or whenever we don't. Though my cravings never get any less for him even though he is just one window away from me, things for him are pretty different. Maybe it would be better if our parents were a little strict and we weren't neighbors in such a pebble-throwing distance. Maybe we should meet as strangers at a friend's party or in a school campaign. Maybe I already ruined a part of it by asking for too much and making myself available to him all the time.

The curtains got closed and now it's the time to come back to reality. Boards' is in two months now and still I couldn't clearly understand why on earth I need to know about the compounds that take part in nucleophilic addition reactions most readily, to get into a college! This is so much of an engineer's thing and opening the chemistry book is the most instant option to get headaches. There should be two different streams for 12th science kids- one for the engineering aspirants, and the other one for the aimless fools like me. I was gonna leave Chemistry after 12th anyway, and this was all Kanishk's stupid idea to get me into this nerd's trouble. I was never meant for science, neither science accepted me as its humble disciple. My interest was always in describing a moonlit night and writing letters to the shooting stars, not making the diagram of sucrose and showing to the examiner how it is a disaccharide.

Ishaan is two years' older than me and he is a college brat now. Sometimes he shares how the college chicks have the same fascination with him just like our high school bitches, and how amazingly he enjoys being in the center of attraction. These tit-talks never instilled any insecurity in me, cause I was always sure that at the end of the day, I was going to get the last slice of pizza. But later I realized how badly I misinterpreted male hormones and their emotions when all the fingers were pointed directly towards me.

After a few days, I finally realized my stupidity for neglecting my studies in the most crucial period of my life, and I was probably gonna let Kanishk win who already questioned my sincerity to bring decent grades that will save my parents from putting their heads down in front of my relatives.

"Nik, I did a terrible thing."- I called Nikhil as my last straw of hope.

"How's that a new thing?"- He was probably in his mid-sleep. So, his sleep-soaked voice didn't show any excitement even after hearing 'Terrible' in a thing. Maybe I am that hideous.

"Shut up! The exam is in two months, and I don't even know the Chemistry syllabus well. Maths and Physics formulae are eating me up. I haven't even opened the Bengali grammar book since the last time I visited tuition. I don't wanna be the clown to be laughed at for failing at her own mother tongue."

"Then open your book and start studying. Why are you disrupting my sleep schedule?"

"Bro, I need your help, else Kanishk's supremacy will force me to be a hobo after results."

"Oh God! Kenny! You are disgusting! When did you get to know that the exam is in two months?"

"From the start of the session."

"So, why the fuck you hadn't studied a bit and disturbing me in the middle of my sleep now?"- His voice was so loud and clear that I was sure if he stayed in my neighborhood, I would probably gonna hear him without the phone.

"Bro, calm down. Let bygones be bygones. I want your help in PCM. I will do Computer and Literature by myself. Please say yes."

Nikhil is my school topper from the day I met him. His rank never went below three, and he is probably gonna be the second IITian I will know. He's also taking help from Kanishk for his JEE preparation, and the last time I talked to him, Kanishk said Nikhil has higher possibilities to get IIT KGP or Delhi, if he doesn't get too unlucky. So, sandwiching between two toppers brings both the perks and timidities on my own. They are definitely helpful but their machine needs a hell lot of oil to process it.

"Fuck your bygones. You were too busy enjoying your teens with those rich hopeless brats, and when reality shut the door on your face, you came to ask for help! Do you think I never noticed that you are bunking classes repeatedly? Do you know what's gonna happen if your mom gets to know about it? I do even know you were fooling around with Ishaan Khandelwal wasting your crucial time for preparation, and you are well aware of that. So, whenever someone is intentionally destroying her own future; who the fuck am I to stop? Do whatever you want, just don't disturb my sleep."

Oh God! He's so brutally right this time, but I don't have any other option rather than being clingy with him until thermodynamics starts seeming a little bit less complicated.

"I am gonna come to your house in the afternoon. We will study optics today and for chemistry, I am leaving it on you. Tell aunty to make some brownies for me. See you soon, Pal...."

"FUCK YOU KENNY!"

I cut the phone and started blowing off the dust from the book covers to have an understanding over the things I was gonna face in the afternoon. At least, I had to be a little less of a loser than Kanishk wanted me to be.

Who says all the endings are painful? End of exams hits me with a better pleasure than a shivering orgasm. This is the time pupils actually try to be productive, learn new skills, go on a trip or get into a relationship and some are sincere enough to clear JEE. I am never at peace with the mindset of IITians. Means how can someone be so sincere not to enjoy their after-boards' vacation and stump their head into books unless the impossible starts seeming possible? When Kanishk was preparing, I didn't have any idea about IITs and the attention it can bring from your fake relatives after you get into it. Kanishk always had a rude and zero-fucks-given attitude towards our neighbors and relatives; so, if he wouldn't clear IIT-B, we would never gonna know the whopping number people who admire him so much. Maybe as a brother, he never succeeded to get my empathy, but as a son, he can be the example for every boy next door.

My exams are finished but Nikhil's JEE is knocking at the door. So, even after having ample opportunities to go out, I can't even call Nikhil unless it's really urgent. I want him to have the best, so I send him regular morning texts motivating him with more power and energy. IIT is a dream that Nikhil molded in his heart from the day Kanishk inspired him to get in. I know he can do it and I believe he will do it.

Most of my evenings pass in front of TV, running through the logic-less Bengali serials with my mom, where all the mother-in-laws somehow try to poison their daughter-in-laws without any reason. First few days, I was watching it because I was trying to do something else rather than finishing off my story books and writing letters to the imaginary astronaut who is stuck on some lonely planet without food and water and waiting for someone to read his SOS and rescue him from his current situation. But after some time, it starts getting less annoying as I fall into its trap of making people addicted. So, I started becoming more of a mumma's girl by hating the same character as intensely as my mom does.

In between, I got a call from Nikhil, which was pretty weird at that time in the evening. So, I picked up his call and properly felt the suppressed excitement through his voice.

"Kenny, have you logged into your Facebook recently?"

"Not in a month, why?"

"I want you to log it in and check Ishaan's profile. Call me afterwards."

"What's in there? What's happening?"

"I want you to look by yourself."

He cut the call without listening to me further. I readily logged into my Facebook and saw Ishaan's updated relationship status with Arunima Sahani where Nikhil Sengupta's like was twinkling along with other thousand likes. I know Arunima through Ishaan. They are college buddies and Arunima's admiration towards Ishaan is unavoidable from the very first day. But I never knew these two were fishing in the deep sea, where I was admiring the bliss it brought me throughout. Ishaan and I haven't been in touch for four months now. Last time we met, I asked for some space as my boards' was approaching and he didn't care to contact me back after my exams were over. Apart from getting a glance from my window, I didn't even talk to him in these months and surprisingly that didn't make me insane. In fact, all the time I lay down on my bed futilely, staring at the ceiling, his thoughts never came across my mind. Maybe I am too saturated with the idea of loneliness now, that I am scared to let anyone in, to invade my inner-peace.

But giving space doesn't mean moving on and finding a new chick. I asked for the space to realize the worth of being distant, being sustainable and wanting him back above all my love for solitude. I never thought Ishaan would find a new way to bless or curse his life. So, I called him and wanted him to take accountability for his depravity.

"Kenny"-His voice didn't sound much remorseful.

"Don't you think you owe me an apology?"

"APOLOGY? For what? For finding someone to love properly? Kenny, grow up. You yourself know that our relationship was at a dead end. I tried to end it a long ago, but thinking about your exam pressure and all, I didn't hurt your feelings. I was being kind to you and you want me to apologize for that! Have you ever tried to read me? Tried to know what I wanted from you? Our relationship was like a failed arranged marriage. Just because you are my neighbor, I tried to make things as good as possible, but from your side it was nothing. No intensity, no intimacy, nothing. Have you ever tried to touch me properly? It was always like babysitting you. We are grown-ups Kenny, try to understand. You never made me comfortable enough to talk about the things I needed between us. You have failed to make me love you. I could never do that. You are terribly insecure about yourself, your mind is always dimming with unearthly imaginations and you want me to be sure about you? I can't do it anymore, Kenny. I am tired of the drama of being a couple when we have nothing in common. I never felt like myself when I was with you. It was always faking to be someone else I am not. I no longer want to do it. I am sorry. If you wish, we can stay friends. "

"What?????...Okay!"

I cut the call. I called him to ask for an apology, but he gave me much more than that- a realization. A realization of being just an entertaining part of someone's drunken nights, when I wanted to be their regularity. I never matter; I never mattered. He showered kindness on me. He tried to adjust for not bringing any toxicity between two neighbors. He tried not to hurt my feelings amid my exam stresses. He almost did everything but to love me.

My phone rang one more time and it was Nikhil again.

"You saw"

"Yup"- In between, mom put a fruit bowl on my table, so I was chewing a grape while his questions hit me.

"You are gonna leave him now?"

"When did I hold him back? I called him and he told me that he was just being kinder to me. There was nothing else. He used to talk about Arunima a lot. Maybe it started from that time. Leave it. Isn't it your revision time? Why the hell are you wasting your time on my baseless love story now?"

"Who doesn't like gossip, right? I was feeling sleepy, so I just opened Facebook to scroll some memes. Thanks to Ishaan for washing out my dizziness. I even read all the comments. Sadly, nobody said anything about you. Hell of a cheat."

"Maybe he didn't say anything about me in his college. I never mattered to him anyway. Not in a mood to talk. Will call you later, Nik."

MY DELICIOUS STRANGER

Summer has arrived in Kolkata, and it's the time to drop down your head to the evening hailstorm and to the sweat popping out from every possible gland of your skin. I always pictured summer as a loyal lover of my city. It meant to part ways for a few countable days of winter, but it comes back earlier than promised. One moment it's bright and breezy, shielded in cardigans and scarves, and the other moment the sweat droplets are running down to your lips. You can escape the humidity in the conditioned air inside your lenient room, but the roads are waiting for you outside, adorning all the moist and the sultry winds. From the richest couch of the luxury cars, to the man who is selling tea in the midday sun, its bewildering disposition of gluing your shirt with sweat and dirt is equal for all. Unless you are a permanent inhabitant here or love this city endlessly for its glory, food and people, Kolkata's humidity will make you lose your mind.

Our results are out, and I am officially a college girl now. Nikhil has done outstandingly well in his JEE and he has got his dream college- IIT KGP. He lives in the campus hostel for five days, comes back home on Friday night and again returns to his hostel on Sunday evening. He's a moody mumma's boy like Kanishk, so staying up there alone on the weekends is still not a thing for him. At first, I was pretty upset to let him go to a new place where he would gonna make a bunch of new friends, and might forget my unimportant influence in his life, but then I consoled my insecurities over the things that needed to be normalized as soon as possible. I do hate Goodbyes but the sooner I will learn to accept them from the people I really care for, the more I will be at peace with myself. The world can't swivel on my way; I should be the one to accept the things it is bringing on me.

Ishaan seems pretty happy with his girlfriend, and it's good to see him finally satisfied in his relationship. Whenever we catch a glance unintentionally, exchanging smiles is the only way to stay humble. Though this bitterness has no effect on the real and loud laughters between our moms, they still talk for infinite hours and exchange hotpots whenever Youtube makes them learn a new recipe.

This is the reason why you shouldn't fall for your neighbor, especially when you are one of the most unwanted, and barely noticeable species on the face of earth, like me. The inescapable awkwardness I need to encounter among all those unwilling eye-contacts which brighten his happiness without me isn't the most comforting thing I want to get at the very beginning of my day. Nikhil told me once that boys never get over their ex, but I do feel that Arunima is probably one of those luckiest women alive who doesn't need to be insecure about her boyfriend's ex. I made Ishaan look for someone better even more. I made him desperate for a valid love, which was never supposed to come from my side. With me, there was no filling him. Whoever gets so lucky to get such an ex-in-law like me?

It was a rainy evening, and I was busy catching raindrops on the lid of my unfinished snack platter when Nikhil buzzed me up. It was a Thursday and he was supposed to come the next evening. So, I didn't see any need to call me, rather he had a very good reason to break my mood.

"Kenny, are you free tomorrow?"

"No."

"Why are you provoking me to be bad with words?"

"What happens tomorrow?"

"I need you to buy a perfume for my mom. Do you remember Saturday is her birthday? I won't be getting enough time to buy anything on Friday night. Will you do that for me?"

"Yes, sure. But how can I know which fragrance she will like?"

"This is a female thing. You must know it better than me. And also you two have the same kind of choices. So, I think whatever you like, mom will like too. So, choose any good fragrance and make it in a gift wrap. I will pay whenever I reach home. Don't fucking break the bottle by your insensibility."

"If you are putting responsibility on me, you have to trust me a little."

"I absolutely don't."

"Oh, you want me to work for you with this tone. God bless you and your expectations on me. I am not doing it, bye."

"Do it for my mom. I will treat you an ice cream. I promise."

"Fine. Any preference for stores?"

"You can get tons in South city. Whatever feels right, take it. Just don't choose anything that comes with the cost of my kidney."

"Will try."

To be very honest, I didn't remember her birthday, which itself aroused a guilty feeling in me. I ought to remember it cause she gifts us a lot of fresh fruits and veggies from her garden, and my mom loves to try new recipes on them. Apart from that, aunty never treated me anything less than her own child, and most importantly, she makes the best brownie in the world. So, I should've put some efforts to make her feel special on her birthday, and there should be something from my side too that can conceal the fault of my absent mind.

The next day, I booked a cab to drop me off at south city mall. It's the distance of a break journey and my lazy ass preferred paying a little more to reach there in the most comfortable way possible. It's a place you should visit when you are in Kolkata. With all the luxury, and semi-luxury brand outlets, this is the estuary where the aesthetic northies and wealthy south Kolkata people meet. The different monotonous vibes from every part of Kolkata dissolves here and become even better and enjoyable for the crowd.

Most of the time I came here, I came alone. Nikhil is the worst shopping companion anyone can ever have. His ugly face of disgust whines around until I am folding my shopping bag to the counter and making a bill as soon as possible. I don't think it's only Nikhil's problem that he can't keep his legs straight in a billing counter but can stand the whole night in front of the TV to shout for his favorite football team. It's a communal problem for every male in this world. They themselves can't choose a matching pair of shoes with their tux, and they are still not ready to cooperate when someone else is doing that part for them. And they say females are complicated; Good Lord!

After wandering around all the fragrance outlets, I finally fixed my mind to a perfume from the Clinique store which cost well enough to wash down every single penny from my wallet. I was pretty sure that aunty was gonna love it as a birthday gift, but there was no assurance that Nikhil would stay right after paying seven thousand bucks for a single perfume bottle. It was a french cologne and had a heavenly fragrance. I sent him a picture of the receipt though but he didn't get enough time to seenzone me. So, I was waiting for the bomb to drop down while booking an Uber pool. It left me with no money after buying the cologne and a drink for me, so, I had to wait for the pool to come and share the trip with some random strangers.

Fortunately, I was its first ride, so I get to choose the window I like avoiding. After 5 minutes of a smooth ride, the car got stuck in jam, and I lost all hopes of reaching home on time. If you have ever been in Kolkata, and stuck in jam near Prince Anwar Shah Road, you have already passed through the hardest patience test of your life. It was my turn then. But somewhere some of my good deeds saved me that day. 'Saved' would be the least appropriate word if I put it before, but something that saved my ass actually brought me into the light of the real darkness of my life.

What could you possibly do when you are stuck at a traffic jam? Wise people read books; modern folks scroll social media and other people stream music while running their mouth. I was sitting there silently fixing my eyes on the traffic surgeon, waiting for him to release the signal. In between, like the first wild wind of a cyclone, a stranger came into my car hurriedly, ordered me to shift a few places with his polite tone, and slammed the door while panting heavily. Rude tones are easy to avoid or replace with a strong reply. But my heart always falls for every sweet behavior I get; even if it's for a hideous job I don't want to initiate. I could easily argue about why he made me move to another seat when I fixed my spot before he came over, but I couldn't. There's something in him that sedated my words. I obediently gave up my comfortable spot with his one request.

When he entered the car, he brought a tantalizing fragrance with him. It was probably a foreign male-perfume; retroactively strong and nerve-wrecking. As the AC was on, the fragrance was increasing every second until it filled up every corner of the car. I even noticed the pool driver was taking long breaths to pleasure his nasal walls. But it was not only his smell that stopped the blinks of my eyes; it was him, when I looked at his face; every pulse of his appearance took my breath away. His sweat-soaked peanut brown hair was falling against his forehead, and the loose-cut sleeve of his innerwear was peeping to demand its existence to the light. Do boys even know they are sexier when they are wet? Means sweaty or watery, whatever!

He rubbed his face with a freshness-wipe, and some sweat droplets were still lingering on his eyebrows, waiting for the AC to dry them. When he spoke out his OTP, I heard him once again. His voice was a true eargasm, and my senses were struggling hard to stay sane against it.

He looked at me once, just for a glimpse, and my eyes witnessed the most wondrous creation the almighty has ever created. His sweat showered t-shirt and ripped blue denim seemed to get some relief inside the comparatively cooler shed of the car. The fragrance started getting mixed with the smell of his sweat making it more flamboyant and drifty to resist.

His shirt got totally glued with his body and now, his abs were more visible and venerable than before. I had never seen such a desiring appeal and an immense exquisiteness in a guy in my whole life. To my overdramatic soul, I was thinking of locking him into my room for a day, and spending the whole time elaborating his machismo in an artsy notepad. If I were a hippie, I would probably use the word *'vintage'* to describe his charm and elegance, but for me he was the last mouthful of brownie, vanilla scope and melted chocolate altogether. You can cherish the smell and taste beyond the time it lasts.

After he came, somehow the maddening traffic was no longer an issue to hate the busy streets. No heat, humidity was bothering me anymore, my eyes were on the rearview mirror, sneaking his face again and again, drawing fascinations upon it. He was like the addictive dizziness on Sunday morning- where prolonged hours lose the battles to those kinder five minutes.

The traffic was stagnant and resentful for everyone, but the outside commotion had no effect on him. He was still as calm as the morning sea and his allure was slowly weighing me into his web of desires. While I was so much into that fangirl moment, my mom's call popped up on my phone screen, and I finally realized it was getting too late than I promised. Neither I could control the traffic, nor I wanted to, so as a responsible daughter I should let her know that I am alive and on a safe way home. But due to my negligence last night, my battery was dying faster than it actually drains, and before I picked up the call, it died, keeping me hanging in the middle. I generally never care to call anyone back unless it's my mom or I am in the middle of somewhere, but She has developed high blood pressure just by visualizing some hypothetical deadly situations on me and Kanishk whenever we fail to pick up her call on time.

So, I had to call her anyhow, before she started preparing herself for my funeral and the only safe option visible was to borrow the phone from my delicious stranger before it got too late.

"Hey, can I borrow your phone for a moment? Mine is dead and I had to call……"- I gathered all the courage and turned them into words.

"Sure."- He handed it over before I finished explaining why I needed a phone from a random stranger, and why I wasn't sensible enough to put my phone on charge before stepping out of the house. And as a freebie, we exchanged smiles for the very first time. The last string of the dam got ripped off from its roll, and the wave of amazement hit me straight. I couldn't hold myself together anymore and a part of me already drifted away to the farthest, from where his smile shines like the most tempting moonlight.

Finally, I talked to mom and gave it back to the owner.

 "Bengali?"- I heard his voice slip into my pitfall. So, I looked at him to confirm if he was really offering me a conversation opener, or I was hearing him babbling just to glorify his presence.

"Ye-a-a-a-ah; Do you?"- Stammering was my situational norm then, and it should be. I realized he patiently heard me talking to my mom and couldn't understand a single word because of the language barrier. My interrogation was baseless. From the moment he got into the cab, I clearly interpreted him as my non-communal boy. Bengal has undoubtedly produced millions of gems and pride, but in my cab, the other part of India was winning over.

"Unfortunately not."- He smiled again. "Maharashtra is my birth place. Have been staying up here for a few months and already fall in love with your city except the perspiration. You can see already."

I didn't expect my stranger to be this chatty, and I absolutely loved how he was making rooms to be less confined. Now, it should be my turn to bounce back the same vibes.

"That's a very non-Bengal problem. We are very much used to it. Every year it comes and goes and brings more humidity along with the rainy winds. You like the monsoon?"

"More than anything."

"Oh wow! Me too. What's your name though?"

"Adithya……Adithya Shanbhog. And you are?"

"Kiyana Mukherjee."

"Bengali surnames are really cool. This place is unique with names."

"Adithya is ours though. It means the sun."

He shrugged his shoulders firmly. Maybe he knew this earlier. After a few moments of silence, he spoke up again.

"My place is nearby, I have to go. Nice meeting you, Kiyana."

I was so dedicated to this colloquialism that I didn't even notice when the traffic was released and how we had arrived at his place so early. After this dreamy fifteen minutes, now I had to go alone for the rest. Maybe good things are so writhing because they are transient. You just only taste a few bites satisfyingly; and before you even start craving more, they are already gone.

"Nice meeting you too."- For the last time, I smelt him a breathful. His smell was so addictive; like the wild storm in a wintery night; both impulsive and enthralling.

This was a badbye. There was no good in it. There were no sequences, no promises, no possibilities to see each other again. Why on earth are there so many gleaming flowers when you aren't allowed to pick one?

He waved me bye from outside until I could see him no more. Suddenly, my thirsts hit me up, I was boiling on my needs; the need of seeing him again, hearing him saying my name, the need of touching him to the core until I am full and saturated. I was clogged, frantic and horny at the same time. He was my turn on. A new name listed in my holy book of indulgence; not a new name-maybe the only name- Adithya. I was pretty sure that my nights were gonna be sleepless for a while.

I came home running from the landmark where my cab dropped me off and started panting desperately at the doors. My t-shirt was so soaked in sweat that it was hard to split over from my skin. Mom left the door unlocked for me, so I just banged it open and hurried up to her room to check Adithya's number in her call list.

But it's my mom, who always deletes unknown stuff from her call history to dial her frequent numbers easily without scrolling down unnecessary junks- the outcome of having infinite free time while watching boring commercials between those bullshit serials.

"Mum, where's the number I called you from."

"What number, Kenny?"- She asked without moving her eyes from her phone screen and I saw my sudden presence didn't make any difference in her Facebook scrolling.

"The number I called you from, from the road. My phone was dead. Where's the number?"- I didn't think my questions convinced her enough to put some attention to it. She was still into her Facebook feed, scrolling pictures and dropping likes.

"Mum…...you're listening to me?"

"Kenny, look, Mr. Agarwal's son is getting married. His wife posted the Mehendi pictures with the family. Don't you think the bride's makeup is a disaster? Means, she looks better with light makeup. We have to attend the wedding next week. I wish our Kanishk was here. His son and Kanishk used to play all the time on our trips, and you used to stay indoors and sit alone with those cartoon shows. Now, his son is getting married, don't know when my Kanishk will settle down."

Mr. Agarwal is my dad's office colleague, and I got to know that day instant, his son was getting married and we already got an invitation.

I sometimes admire my mom's zero-fucks-given-to-other's-opinion attitude and how amazingly she ignores to listen to others when she has a tight gossip. For that moment, I didn't give a fuck if Mr. Agarwal's son was getting married or having a divorce. All I needed was that number to build the bridge between harsh reality and my dreamy desires.

"Mum, what the hell! I am asking for that number and you are not even paying a little attention to me."

"Don't you dare to talk to me with that tone! Is this what you are learning from college? And why are you sweating like this? Take the water from my table."

I finished the glass at a moment and again started whimpering about the number.

"What number, Kenny?"-She asked again and now she finally looked at me with a rapid disgust in her face.

"Mum, my phone was dead in the middle of the road and I took someone else's phone to call you. So, I need that number."

"But Kenny, I deleted it after cutting your call. This isn't new. Why do you need that number so badly?"- I didn't know either to let the anger burst out on her or to find a plausible answer to what she had asked. It was the last piece of hope left for me, to build a string by which I could again see him, and hear him closely. It all died at a glance. I was so over with everything.

I left the question unanswered and came back to my room empty-hearted, deranged in anger and numbed by tiredness. It was the first time, my driftwood had stopped for someone, my desires found perfection and my longing was touching the rooftop. The feeling was rare and new. It was something I never felt for Ishaan. This was probably the spark he used to ask for, about which I never felt like finding it for him. And when I actually felt the need, suddenly it was so very useless. It felt like I was stuck in a staircase where both the ends were opened to the dark; without glinting any ray of hope. It doesn't matter if it's Adithya or Ishaan, men are way out of my league.

After half an hour of plug-ins, my phone came back to life and showed 3 missed calls and 7 Whatsapp text notifications from

Nikhil. Now, I had to call him back and elaborate on why I couldn't go for a cheaper choice and why women are so dumb to spend an enormous amount on the thing that is hardly noticeable.

"Hey, Kenny, off to the world, good to hear you are alive."

"Shut up, I rang first, I speak first. Let me clear the cloud. I tried to find all the alternate options, but trust me some of them smelt like Ramen. I know aunty doesn't like strong smells, so this was the best fit in if I tick all the preferences. And the fragrance is heavenly, I promise you will love it too. You can use it sometimes."

"You realize that's a ladies' perfume, right."

"Nope, it's a cologne."

"How the hell is that a different thing? And fucking seven thousand bucks! I should have chosen someone else. You are just as dumbass you were before."

"Last year, you spent over 30k for your PS4. So, what's wrong with it? If you can't afford it, we can share the price. I was thinking about gifting her something, so we can manage that from here."

"Unless I have to pay the whole, I am okay with everything. But why was your phone off? You forgot it there?"

"It was dead, I forgot to charge before stepping out. You know, I met a guy today, and I think some parts of me are really into him. He was really handsome and…."- I took a pause.

"And………I don't know, he was kinda turn-on for me."

"It happens to everyone. It's just the hormones talking. I will see you on Saturday. Have classes to catch up. Bye now."

Like everyone else in the world, my feelings are so invalid to him too. Like my parents, my brother, my so-called friends, no one ever tries to listen to me, about how I feel, how I see things, the sunsets, the cloudy nights, how I listen to the goodbyes, and the fake promises. It was all alone mine. In my school years, I spent most of the days trying to fit in and not proving myself as a loser. Everyone was running on their minds, where I was just being distilled in the fear of being left alone. Among all the bffs I made in my school life, only Nikhil survived as the fittest. For the other friends, mostly the females I befriended once, backstabbed me so highly, that whenever I heard someone's praising about the bffs, it resonates with me as betrayal-flattery-forever.

THE LOST CALL

"*Kenny*, your phone."

It was a lazy Sunday. I was lying back on bed, my one hand was on the half-opened college textbook resting upon my chest, another was busy scrolling my Instagram feed and drowning deep into the trap of those hilarious memes. In the past few days, I tried to find Adithya on every possible social media I have. I hacked Nikhil's LinkedIn account as I don't have one, to look for anyone named Adithya Shanbhog, but it seemed like he had just gone with the wind. Nikhil is always the dumbest about passwords. Other than NikDasgupta123, he can never imagine putting some complicated typos to trick those jobless hackers.

All the Adithyas I found were no him. And this fresh-out failure of finding him back, accelerated my enticement to keep up with the manhunt thousand times more. But unless I was surviving that number anyhow or destiny kindly dropped him off on my doorstep, there were no possible chances to see him again. I know we were in the same city, breathing the same air, but the leading footsteps were undeniable too.

In between, I heard mom yelling from her room downstairs.

"It's in my hand, mom."- My voice was loud enough to wake up the dog sleeping peacefully, straight down to my window.

"Someone is looking for you on my phone, come on down. He is speaking Hindi. I can't understand." – I know it's hard for a Bengali to communicate in Hindi with someone so efficient, and my mom never showed any kind of interest in learning that language and being coherent with Hindi-speaking people. Her dedication towards monolingualism forcefully made our so-called sophisticated neighbors speak Bangla. She is never wrong though. Bengali is the utmost comfort to your throat.

"Why don't you learn to speak Hindi?"- I was obviously annoyed for making me come downstairs after being so comfortable in bed.

"Why do you give people my number to contact?"- Winning an argument with my mom is the Oxford definition of IMPOSSIBLE. Even my dad and my IITian brother always surrender themselves towards this female supremacy; so who the fuck I am to hold a chance!

I came down and blankly took the phone without looking up to the number, thinking it must be from an affiliate marketing agency.

"Hey Kiyana, it's Adithya, we met a few days ago; in a cab, you remember?"

Within a few seconds, my faceful of disgust turned into a shy smile, my fingers stuck as I was playing with, flipping over and over, and my throat ran out of moist. The voice- the deep, condescending, manly voice. The voice I was praying to hear every single day since I met him. A lightening frolicked through my body and I couldn't help but feel the flood of adrenalin crushing through my veins. My hormones were at bombardment, and nothing can be holier than my excitement of getting him back and seeing that face again.

"Hi, anybody there?" – He asked again.

"Yes, yes……umm……this is Kiyana, how are you?"- That time anyone could feel the shaking exhilaration in my voice.

"It's been a week. I thought you might forget."

I took a deep breath and smirked on my own. Really? Forget? Like he left me with an option to forget! What's worth forgetting? His face? His voice? His smell? I am probably taking them to the grave.

"Hey, I haven't forgotten anything. But…….. Wait, I am calling you from my number. This actually belongs to my mom. So, ……"

I tried to keep my expressions as uniform as possible, so that my face of revulsion successfully eludes my mom's eyes.

"I won't call here." -He finished my sentence.

"Yup, wait a minute."- I cut the call, and readily by hearted his number from digit to digit.

"Who has called?"- Mom didn't look very eager to know.

I wish I could tell her "Your son-in-law", but I controlled my tongue in fear of getting scolded badly.

"Kanishk's friend. He was asking for his new number"- I lied.

Lies aren't really the section of my expertise. For me, it is an art for the smart folks. I had seen Kanishk lying without any hesitation after eating my tub of ice cream and licking the leftovers lingering around his lips while I was watching him. He used to lie to mom every vacation about not coming back home and spent nights with a bunch of strippers or sometimes escorts hovering around his hotel room in sexy lingerie. Kanishk's roommates used to put those videos in Whatsapp status and never cared to hide me as they already knew I was never gonna tell their parents what actually happens when you put a bunch of horny engineers together with the burden of assignments and never-ending syllabus, away from their home, high and dry. Among all of them, my brother was the groundbreaker, and the other ones were his silent and dedicated devotees. He is a true man of mischief.

"So, Kenny! Right? I hope this number belongs to you at least."

"Yah, this is mine, and you can call me Kenny too."- I smiled.

"So, how are you doing these days?"

"Pretty good, I hope you are good too."

"Yup."

A fear passed through my mind as I didn't know how to keep myself up with the conversation. I always suck at making conversation when the person is new and I am unfamiliar with his mind. This is the reason I never signed up on any online dating app in fear of being regular with those fuzzy texts and being rated in their scale of judgments where I hardly stand a chance to be the one. Even when Ishaan and I were dating, we used to talk once in a week, mostly about our own household things where there was nothing but boredom. For him, I could never be the girlfriend who would spend nights talking to him over any baseless topic and send my pictures in lingerie or sometimes nothing when he is in a mood to pleasure the man down him.

I always choose peace over drama, mystery over rut and sleep over anything else, and he made good use of my generosity by finding a suitable partner where I was trying to find the missing pieces of the puzzle that could possibly fix us together. But when he left, it didn't change me at all, it actually made me realize how severely I am made to be alone, to be myself.

In my college days, I mostly sat alone in the library when my other mates used to stay busy collecting opinions on where to go for lunch that could make everyone happy. During the classes, my immediate neighbor's desks used to stay empty unless it was a day of mandatory attendance. No one chooses me to be their friend, unless I initiate things and later be at gunpoint when their betrayal hits me down. So, not being able to pair up a conversation with someone I like, is my behavioral disability, and I never tried to get rid of it.

"So, Adithya, what makes you call me again?"- There was a part of me still wondering if it was happening in real! It seemed like a mirage of getting his call so at a time when I was fantasizing him 24x7.

"I was wondering if I could make some friends here. As I am totally new, your name comes to my mind first. So, I thought of calling you. Wasn't sure, though, if it was your mom's number."

"I am so glad you called. Don't you have any friends here?"

"I do, but they are also like me, staying for a while. Don't belong to this land."

"Have you seen the famous places here? It was the capital of British India."

"Yah, I know. I stay quite busy these days, so, didn't get enough time to go out. You are in college right? Where's your college?"

"Ballygunge. You know about it?"

"My place is very near to Ballygunge. Maybe we will come across someday again."

"Sure"

Shouldn't he be saying we would meet someday sooner, or something that could end up the line between the dreams and the reality? Hearing his voice was never enough when he was under the same sun and my legs could afford traveling to him.

After the call got disconnected, I started planning new excuses to call him again, just to hear his voice, maybe hear him saying my name or anything that could make us see each other again. I was too dumb to ask about his whereabouts- where he lives, what he does, who he is actually! He was so sudden like his call that I couldn't convince myself to brush up on my poor socializing skills and my breaths were still desperately longing for curbing up the excitement. Maybe I should call him one day and make sure that he gets to know everything I wanted to say but could never speak up about, or maybe I should leave the whole Adithya-Fantasy behind and stride back to my old friend- me, myself and I.

Last Wednesday, our HOD gave us some assignments and, as Nikhil was here one day more than usual, he helped me finish them all in a single day. So, I came to college today to submit them and get a signed copy for my semester exam practicals. Our HOD was quick and he seemed pretty impressed to have me done with the assignments earlier than others, who were always over-dramatic with their refined oiling skills to get more attention and appreciation for being regular in class.

"Good job, Mukherjee. Finally you are taking interest in the syllabus rather than making doodles on the last page of your notebook."

I wonder how he got to know that I make stupid doodles on the last page which is actually the uncorroborated doodle page from every notebook company to nourish the artists inside every worthless student like me. His words comfort me a little. Getting praises is never a regular thing for me, and when I finally get something as precious as honest praise, I remember it to every word. These are some peanut happiness that helps me keep breathing even at the toughest situation.

After getting the signed copy, I come to the orchard to spend some quality hours with the flowers and their loving bugs before starting off for home. There's a huge banyan tree standing proudly in the very middle of the orchard, highs to the sky, boughs down to the earth, and enrooted deeply to another world of darkness. For me, this tree has always accepted me to be in its consortium when my other mates just passed judgments why I never initiate conversation with them. When I finish off this college, all I am gonna remember is the tree and the dusty bench left alone to the right corner of the orchard. Nobody goes there except me when I strongly want not to be seen. That place belongs to me unofficially. I clear the bench when I am in a mood to sit there and write something unearthly. I sometimes water those little twiggy groves when Kolkata is pouring fire on earth bringing down the sun. This tree has witnessed a lot of scenes. Our physics professor once said it has been here since independence, maybe a little before that. It has seen all the prolapses in British India as well as the annihilation of socialism in the name of the modern era. I wish I could talk to the trees, listen to its stories, fears, and nourish it before mourning on my life. Maybe there's a spirit hidden inside- a life, a thought, a heartful of kindness. I bet trees are better friends than humans even at their utmost silence. If it could talk, I would definitely share my stories. The stories of my failures, my regrets, and sometimes about the adjustments I never wanted to make. Also about the last time I met Adithya and how it made stars dance through my skin- all. Maybe it would listen to me and wouldn't think I was insane, unlike others.

I sat down leaning against its bark which was quite clear and free from bugs. I was thinking about being in this serene environment for a pretty long time as there wouldn't be any chances of getting late within those fresh pastel shades of the sky that didn't even hit past 9 in the morning. As it's pretty early from official college hours, not a bustle was crowding over here and there. This was the perfect place to write about Adithya which I had been thinking, for a long time. Therefore I reach out to my spiral notebook and let my pen hopping on whatever I was thinking I could write.

"I met him on my way where destiny brought some twists over pain. He was like the cloudy winds carrying the first essence of the monsoon, with a relief of rain after a deadly drought. I couldn't think of……..."

"A deadly drought, huh! Kenny, you write too?"

While writing, I didn't notice that a tall, wide shadow lowered his head to my notebook pages, to sniffle or to observe, probably. When he spoke up, I just felt his breath whistling around my ears and suddenly, my thoughts just scattered like glass pieces. I gazed up at him, and my glance stuck on his unruffled face. It was Adithya, the canvas I was drawing my words on. For some time, I thought maybe my notebook has some magical power to bring in life on whatever I write, but then I actually realized I was too old to believe in witchcraft and wizardry. Harry Potter is only satisfying in movies, there's no professor Snape out there to save me.

"Wait! Whaaaat! How did you come here? How do you even know I am here? I didn't hear you coming."- My face filled with a wholesome smile mixed with wonders of an unexpected reality.

"I tapped my feet silently."- He smiled back.

"But how do you know I am here?"- I echoed.

"Do you believe in magic?"- His face was firm, confident and unattended about the surroundings.

"No………..I don't think there's anything like magic."

"Then you are mature enough. I saw you through the little block in the gateway. You know you are sitting exactly one eighty degree with the main entrance. Whoever gets in, can have a first glance at you, if he wants."- In between he sat beside me leaving two, three inches gap, at an untouchable distance between our knees.

His appearance was still a mystery to me though, but my words fall short when he is around me. I hardly find things to talk about that won't make me look like a dumb in front of me. Also, I want him to keep talking. Talk as long as he wants me to listen, as long as I am able to hear the sound of the doorbell; I just don't want him to stop. His voice is the utmost pleasure to my ears.

 "You still don't understand how I got here, right?"

I smiled with my eyes.

"I told you, I stay nearby. I came to the departmental store to do some shopping. On the way, I saw you crafting something in here. So, I thought of paying you a visit. Your college people are liberal though. They allow visitors anytime."

"Yah, the regular hour will start in an hour, they won't allow anyone then without an id card. Before and after, people often come here to visit this orchard. It's too big to get crowded."

"Oh, I see. Do you come to college regularly?"

"As regular as a full moon night."- I said. "Where do you stay exactly? This area?"

"Next alley, 4 minutes running distance from this place."

"This is a people's area. You can't get a moment alone here."

"That's not totally true. Just like I got a moment here with you, it was all of a sudden. My landlord is kinda like you, doesn't like to get along with people. So, my place is quiet all the time. By the way, do you write often? Am sorry, I sneaked into it. But I swear it was unintentional."- I was utterly enthralled to see him noticing the silence of my moral turpitude.

"It's absolutely okay. Even though it's the first time somebody actually read my writing. You don't need to be sorry about it. "

"Can I read some more? I loved the way you initiated the paragraph."

His words echoed to my ear several times. I looked up directly at his face. It didn't seem joking and being sarcastic or something I was interpreting wrong. This was the very first time somebody actually showered some kind of interest in my writing. My writing skill was always worthless to everyone unless it was the time to write essays for Nikhil's school project or official letters for any emergency purpose. No one has ever cared to read them once after I wrote and all my servings were wasted in those big junk piles of unwanted papers that might have been eaten up by bugs now.

As I played both the parts of a reader and the writer, I never cared of rescuing those finalized paragraphs from the rough work to my fresh notebooks. This was the perks of lacking, which left with no judgments, no flattery, no extra eyes on them.

"It's kind of a mess. I bet you can read my words from all those crisscross doodles and overwriting I made in my notebook."

"I wish you could give me some light. Never mind. I think it's getting late for you, you should start off if you are done with the college things. Do you think it's gonna rain tonight?"- He squeezed his eyebrows and made his face a little upwards to take a wider view of the sky. It can rain today. A pastry piece of dark cloud is sailing decisively mostly in the north side. If it enlarges into a big bombshell, the night is gonna be a better time to write about him. So, I closed my notebook and said, "It better rain at night. I think it can happen today."

"Really, it will be a relief. If you are planning to get up now, then I can accompany you for a few more steps. You are gonna take the metro?"- I wonder how he can read my mind so brilliantly. I was actually planning to pack up and leave before the college folks started walking in. So spending a few more minutes with him would be like the pleasure of licking the last melted foams from a finished ice-cream cup- the more I get is better.

He matched my footsteps to the main gate and I was followed by his smile till my cab arrived. The afterglow of his arrival was so strong that I wanted a smooth ride to cherish and reverse back all the things he told and find out if there was anything he meant and I didn't catch it for the moment.

He waited there till I got into the cab and then he proceeded towards more left. He was in his house-boxer and a scoop-neck t-shirt that wasn't a very outdoor outfit for a southie, so he wasn't going to socialize much. All the way back home, I was thinking of him being so kind to me. He came to say hello when he could just ignore and go on with his work. He spent some of his busy morning moments with me rather than just thinking it as a waste. He showed interest in my writing when I never felt it could catch an extra pair of eyes, ever in my whole life. This morning is not ordinary. He made it precious for me.

I went back home tired of sitting by the window and visualizing the things we could've done if I were a little bit more expressive. Mom offered a fruit bowl piled with some sweetest mangoes and berries, and I took it to my desk. The view outside my window was deep yellow, and whoever hasn't seen this yet, probably can't understand how yellow can be the royalest of the royals leaving the black behind. With the sky and its molten lava shade, somewhere my gaslit thoughts were kindling inside. His words were making me think if I should start keeping a fresh notebook for real with all the finals or I should keep making the instants into a draft box. Not only for him, it would be easier for me too, if I start being clearer in presentation. It might increase my interest in reading it more; but what if I ain't productive enough to maintain it and stock it up in my wardrobe corner and forget till the pages get yellow and cranky! This has happened to me before and my laziness takes over everything as follows. So, the fear is real.

At night, it was supposed to rain after an overcasted evening sky. But it didn't. So, I straight jumped into my bed with my math book and class copy to finish off the indefinite integral chapter in one night. I love doing calculus as there's no spiral words pounding on my head that can differ from mind to mind. But if I see the overview, math is never boring, even sometimes it works as a healer in place of writing, when my mind declares a shutdown, and I think I am never gonna write again.

The real time lapse happens when I get stuck in some. An hour is worth one face lift and sometimes more. But these hours are enjoyable, away from crossing over any other things in mind and getting satisfaction when the answer key readily matches with your solution. I kind of finished one fourth of my chapter exercises when I heard a message tingling on my phone. It was 1:20 by clock and nobody actually texts me this late. So, when I switched on the screen, I saw it's from Adithya.

Are you inside?

The question was incomplete. Inside of what? What he is trying to mean by inside. But I can't write so many messages altogether, so I only sent,

I am home.

The back text came in a few seconds.

Can you come to your balcony?

The question splitted my world apart from what I created all by keeping my mind focused only on my textbook pages. For a few moments, I thought he was just joking with me at night to see if I am awake or in my mid-sleep. Nobody can ignore a text like that if get in a sense, so maybe it was a test or a truth wrapped in some possibilities.

I didn't go to the balcony first, I peeped over my window. His presence was as intense as the sun- a six-feet-two tall frame in a v-neck quarter sleeve t-shirt, standing right below the light post. His interrogative eyes, looking here and there, probably were trying to get me at a glance. The color of his t-shirt forgathered with the dark surroundings, couldn't find if it was gray, black or any independent color. There was something in his hand, seemed like a paper bag and still my guessing power was struggling to find out why.

I went to the balcony, and it took him a few moments to figure out my presence. He waved at me and then started typing something on his phone.

My mind was still at a war, why he traveled almost 27 kilometers in a peach dark night to see me out of the balcony. I was obsessed with him, but I wonder what's the deal from his side. He never hid his interest in me from the moment we met, but as far I know the nights are saved for the lovers. This is the time your heart craves for a human, a warmth, a support, a listener. Not everyone can be your night. It takes a lot to be in it.

The text hit my display in seconds.

Can you come down? If it's possible.

There was no option as 'No'. I had to go, anyhow, crossing all the barriers. This was the night anyone can ever dream of having, and it was actually happening to my sane self.

Wait a minute- I texted back.

I saw him lifting up his face from the phone and greeting me with a thin smile. I again texted

Come to the back door, I can't go to the light.

Some of my neighbors are terribly insomniac and disgusting. So, if they notice me sneaking out there with an unknown male identity, I would be in house-arrest the next day. So, I changed my clothes in a moment and tapped my feet as silent as possible to reach the back door. Our back door is at a rapid distance with the room where my parents sleep. So, I wore a sock to avoid the sticky noises and tried to flee illusively like a spirit in the thin air.

"Hey, what are you doing here at this time of night? People will talk, you know."

"Do you care about people that much!"- He squeezed his eyes in a dominating way. "I came here to give you something, a very legit thing. I think you need this the most for now."

He flung a paper bag around his elbow and now he widened its mouth to take out a square kind of thing, weighty enough to make his palm down a little bit. He handed it over to me.

"It's for you."

First few minutes, I looked at his face emptily, thinking I must be sleep-walking or hallucinating him in real, but seeing me awestruck like that, he took my hand and placed the thing right there so it didn't fall down. I got a tight grasp and finally made sure that it was a notebook- a hardcover spiral notebook with a cover filled up with *'From the best thinker to the best writer'*.

I spent half of my childhood listening to *'Don't take anything from a stranger, especially any food. Ignore him in a way so he doesn't get hurt.'* Even my mom still keeps reminding me every time I go outside ignoring the fact that nobody ever offers me anything, so that I have a chance to say *'no'*. But for him, it was different. He was neither a stranger, nor a heartlocker to take me away. He was thoughtful- about my passion, about my likes, like the way nobody had ever been. In the morning, he said he needed me to keep a fair copy and at night he came up to my door with a fair copy for my draft box. How can I define this feeling? Dominance? Care? Support? Or a strong will to better my shitty life? Nobody ever cared to manage enough time to take an interest into my life; how I live it, if I barely live it. Even my parents don't have any idea about my notebooks, scattered words inside them; the handful of stories I write every time somebody hurts my feelings; the empowered characters and how they pawn others when they are way too grumpy and get validated by the society for their trail of achievements. A writer's mind can't unsee anything. It observes, it thrives, it cries and burns like hell.

"Do you like the design? It's the best I found in the store. If you don't......"

"I love it. This is thoughtful. I don't know how I can thank you enough for thinking this much about me and buying me the most amazing gift. Thank you. I will keep it safe."- My voice broke down and my eyes got teary.

It was the very first and the most thoughtful gift I ever got. People randomly buy me stupid coffee mugs, and comic books in my birthday that I barely make into use. They hardly think about me while buying. They just pick anything up that's not adultery and fit in their budget easily. Who cares if I read those or it ends up in the minivan of our local ragman! I was emotional this time, for him, to think about me and my writings to this extent, and buy me a thing that is useful and heart-melting. I felt like crying, clearing all the heaps of sorrows inside my heart, but I couldn't. I just thanked him partially and concealed the part where I went down.

"You're happy. Look at you. Your eyes are glittering. I didn't mean to make you cry though. Your eyes are so big and beautiful to be in tears. Look, I have bought chocolate for you. Can you please shove off those tears now?"

His hand again dug deep into the bag and got out with a big chocolate bar. I couldn't be any happier for those moments and already started cherishing some before it was even gone. A longing, a diffused longing for a companion, and a hope for having someone who can be the warmth in the ice-cold heart of the world, shielded me all over. He was watering my ideas of forming perfection in a human.

"Why are you doing this for me? I hardly did a single thing for you?"- I looked at his face and waited to see if anything changed after my interrogation.

"Just felt like doing. I don't believe in doing it to get something in return."- His face didn't change a bit.

I carried the chocolate and the notebook and stood still, waiting for him to speak first. It was not that we used to talk often. Even after he was right there in my Whatsapp and Telegram, I was never brave enough to press the send button after typing a huge message for him. All my texts surrendered back way home in the tempting cave of the backspace. If he ever noticed, he might have seen 'typing' under my name, but those typed texts never made it to him as I didn't get enough confirmation whether it would be a great idea or not. His first text came asking me to come downstairs, else there wouldn't be any colloquiality to see him in my chat's page.

"Got some time?"

"Huh….yah"- The silence made me lost in it.

"There's a place nearby, let's go. I want to show you something."

"Okay."- I couldn't find any other word to place it there. The fear of getting caught for escaping the night with someone I hardly knew was no bigger than my will to have his consortium. His presence made me vulnerable, zesty and happy. There were no options I could choose to go back.

Now, I noticed he came by a car. I never knew he possessed a car, neither had I heard the approaching sound of it nearby. It was a kind of a family car, not too big, not too small, and didn't look like it's his. Moreover its West Bengal number plate and the totally used and dusty condition was revealing it had been in a static position for a long time. So, I rolled my eyes all over and asked, "It's your car?"

"Of course not, why would I buy a family car in this city where I hardly have chances to get a single person for a drive? It's my landlord's. He no longer uses it, so I have the permission to take it anywhere."

"Good for you. He must be a kind-hearted man."

"He does. Come over mine someday. You can meet him there."- He said while starting the engine.

Why someday? Why not today or anytime sooner? I want to go there. I want to meet everyone he knows, his landlord, his parents, his friends, everyone! I want to know everything that possibly interests him, flickers a fire in his heart- like an admirer. He's so near to me, and I want to read him inside out, over all the dark and the light, through every thick and thin, like a novel with enormous pages.

The car stopped near Simon's lake. I didn't know this place existed unless I saw the shimmery cemented letters curved on the entry gate. That's not a proper lake, it was kind of a garden with scattered chairs and benches and some clearly maintained trees and orchards. I didn't think so many people would come here, especially the children, else there would have been chips, biscuits, and plastic bottles everywhere.

We walked in there like the holy shadows and I reached a wide swing following him in the dark. He patted the place offering me to sit and I sat down keeping a hand-fitting distance. The place was visibly shady all around, and the essence of the rain in the wind was palatable with every inch of the skin. The swing we sat, was slinging from a rusty chain. It wasn't swinging at all, but it wasn't claiming the scratching sound as sharp as the nails on a chalkboard. We were silent. My designer clog was touching the ground and I was trying to draw a V without any reason. Maybe because it was the easiest letter to draw with feet or I was trying to avoid eye-contact in fear of saying something silly.

"You see the star?"- He broke the silence after a few minutes.

I looked up to the sky and saw something that I didn't expect to see on a rainy night. Though it didn't rain that night, the sky was sultry with some serious cloud grudges, and a star that night was really the rarest thing I could believe to see. But it was there; alone, heathen, but shiny, sprinkling glitters to moor the foliage, a little less raunchy.

"Yah, it is amazing, stars in a cloudy night."- My words rested for a smile. "Thanks for bringing me here. I will remember this forever."- I said.

He took a deep breath and looked at me scrutinizing my inner-feeling while exhaling it. It was a test, to see if I was really happy or making it up to flow with the mood. Not all people can realize the temptation of watching the stars at a monsoon-midnight. He was checking if I was one of those sleepyheads to choose sleep over the rarest view of stars.

"I will take you there one day, to that star. I love this one. It follows my eyes every night."

I stepped my face forward and widened my smile. "I would love to go there."

"Adithya is too regular, would you mind if I call you Adith?"- I didn't remove my eyes from his face. It's a comfort to see him endlessly, to hear his long breaths and sometimes his humming in some unknown tunes, so close to fuel the desire of touching his fingers, his eyes, the entire unfiltered him; but the universe has some other plans for me.

"Wow, I think I would love to be called Adith. It's better than Adithya."- He seemed happy with the new name. "I think you are thoughtful. I assume I give the right gift to the right person. Keep me in some of your pages."

Some of my pages? I am gonna name every page on you, I will spread your name across the stars, I will dance the city and alleviate the evening by singing your name, I will shrill to the sky and make the clouds clamoring for you. I am yours, Adith; for this moment, for the decade, for the end of the time. I will always be; it doesn't matter if you ever become mine or not. I am all yours and you don't need to know about it.

THE FRIENDLY INVITATION

The memories of last night haven't stopped haunting me to sleep. I came back at almost 3:10, and spent the rest of the dawn imagining him beside me both in a sexual and non-sexual way. At 9am, mom discovered me in my room sleeping like a log, after calling a dozen times from downstairs and not getting any response from my side.

She woke me up with her soft and gentle hand and asked if I was feeling right for sleeping in this unusual hour. I comforted her with my lies of spending the night with some serious calculus problems and got confirmed that none of my parents knew where exactly I was last night. It was my first escape trial, and I succeeded perfectly.

She kept my muesli bowl on my study table and left the door half-opened. I first unplugged the charger and checked his WhatsApp last seen. It was clocked at 3:50 last night. So, either he hadn't woken up then or he hadn't got enough time to check his phone. After a few minutes of thought, I finally sent him a text saying, "Thank you for last night. I will never forget that."

The message doesn't get double-ticked. He is probably asleep. I quickly change his contact from *Adithya* to *Adith*. It's the small piece of possession that makes me the richest of all. He is Adithya to the world, but his Adith is all for me.

The reply came after an hour when I was munching on my peanut butter and muesli bowl after brushing and cleaning myself off for the morning.

"I am glad that you like it. If you ever feel sad, call me. I will take you there."

The text itself is a healer. Nobody ever offers to text them if I feel sad or take me somewhere that I would possibly like to go. My parents try to offer some of my favorite foods if they get any slight indications about my melancholy and feel that I need some care, even if I don't; but that's no longer an effective solution for a 19-year-old. If I ever try to elaborate things precisely, I will end up getting nothing but judgments after a certain point of time. So, I better be left alone and it's not fair to expect them to be more contributory than they have already been. They have grown me up this big and that doesn't make them responsible for my frustrations towards life. I never been a fit-in child for them, I don't have an IIT degree that they can be proud of, I am good for nothing and no skills possess me for making me one in a million, I never get to be the sister my brother wants, I can never become a little one percent brilliant as he is, as he always wants me to be, I am terribly insecure about everything in life, mostly myself and can't make through the dark tunnel to see the ultimate source of light at the end of it - it's all on me. It's my fault that I can't be the version of me everybody would appreciate. I can't be the perfect I want and it's never their responsibility.

"Sure."- I stopped a few moments before sending it. It might be a very short reply for a lovely message like this. "I have my college foundation day tomorrow. I will be out after that. So, if you are free tomorrow, would you love a ride with me?"

He isn't online. His last scene matches the time of his last text. I move on to my stretch sessions and a bit of morning workout. But somehow my mind is stuck there- in his textbox. Even after every one-minute stretch, I am rolling my eyes to see if there's any reply or any *Typing* showing. For some moment, I thought he would say no or just put me on seenzone. It may be too early to ask out even though we spend some night moments together watching stars and naming them for a future living. But what if it was just an insomniac night for him and all he could connect is me cause I am always bad at saying *'no'* and anyone who knows me for a day, can get the essence how pathetic I am for this world.

I draw my chair forward and lean back on the soft cushion comfortable enough to gather all my thoughts for writing. I kept the notebook and the chocolate covered safe in my drawer so that it doesn't catch any eye just in case my parents care to invade my room. The velvet-covered notebook seems to me like Tom Riddle's diary, same in length and width, but with new fresh pages and the inhaling semblance of untouched paper. I open the first page through the spiral binding, and see he wrote *"for Kenny"* in some tempting cursive. It is not too big and deep, and written in just one stroke of the pen. Unless you are turning on the first page intentionally, it's hard to notice that it's even there.

I take a moment to appreciate the fact that he took so much time of his day to buy the notebook and chocolate and later wrote some on the first page, so that my thoughts just don't follow the void tunnels. At least, this is what my mind wants me to interpret. For me, this is the *Koi-No-Yokan*; the Japanese form for the premonition of love- the love only I felt, with the heart wrapped in obvious wildness, through the eyes I find the serenity in him.

In between, my phone's display lit up with the soft tinkle of WhatsApp notification. It's him. I go after the blue-ticked craving zone immediately by letting him know how desperately I was waiting for his reply. I may make myself a little less groovy here, but if it's a *yes*, it will be worth everything.

"Sure thing. Let me know the time a little before."- Thank God, it's a Yes!

"Meet me in front of the parking lot at 11:30; I will be in a Black Sedan."

"Okay"

I run towards the kitchen hurriedly, cause this is the one of the most generalized places to get mom when she is home, skipping one extra stair at a time and almost fall by my heel at the very last one. I got a sprained ankle and it starts paining more when I actually start walking. My pace gets affected and the little hobbles in my walk are unavoidably visible. I try to make it up to mom without letting her know that my stupidities somehow manage to hurt me again and this time it's more physical.

I find her there ladling fish curry in the saucepan. Seeing me in a place where I possess no interest, some little wonders arise in her face.

"I am not frying any nuggets for you, so what else?"

"Mom, can I borrow dad's car for tomorrow? I will come back sooner."

"No!"- She keeps on the ladling, while putting on some other species, which makes her busy enough not to look at me even if I am trying hard to convince.

"Mom, please, for one day. You know I am a safe driver. I took you to aunt's place twice and you have to say those were comfortable rides. Why not now? Come on! Just tomorrow, please!"

"Kenny, a no means a no."

"Please, mom, please, for tomorrow only. Please say yes."- I am not ready to lose so fast.

"Why do you need it tomorrow so bad? What's tomorrow?"

"It's the foundation day of college, so…….I will be back very early."

"So, you will be there to show-off your horrible driving skills."

"Yeah, a little bit. Everybody is coming by their own vehicles, so why take the metro when I can drive myself there?"- I lied. Nobody was bringing their vehicles. Even if they do, that will be nothing but a coincidence. I don't even know if anyone is coming tomorrow either. "And hey, my driving skills aren't horrible. Admit that, I can drive and your son doesn't."

"I told your dad a million times not to get you a license. Nobody listens to me in this house."- She seems pretty annoyed, but the face doesn't get any wrinkles of annoyance yet.

"So, is that a yes?"

"Who are you taking there? Got any company?"

"Nope, all alone."- I lied again.

"So, rather than showing off these useless things, better try brushing up your social skills and make good friends there! Whatever, this is the first and last college car ride for you. You will get the key in the evening. Go to your room now."

I prance a little and stop as soon as my sprained ankle reminds me not to. I kissed her cheeks and went towards my room slowly, trying to make it look like a perfectly normal walk.

"I highly doubt your happiness."- I hear mom yelling from the kitchen, addressing me being so happy, just for allowing a ride. It's doubtful but at least I am happy.

Conclusion: Even if you are getting the permission, you can hardly win over my mom. She is beautiful, interesting, and hard to induce easily. I wish I could be like her one day.

Even though it's just a ride, I spend about an hour in front of the mirror. Today, I solemnly realize how backdated I am from those fake and filtered Instagram influencers. Last night, I shattered two whole hours learning how to do sober makeup, and in the morning, it's all in vain. I do whatever I could possibly do and tried to look into the mirror through someone else's eye, maybe through Adith's eye. Just like, if I were him I would appreciate this face or not.

He said my eyes are big and beautiful. So, I am trying to figure his *beautiful* among these fuss of brown skin, thin lips, sharp nose and beyond those big and agile eyes. It's not surreal that my admiration seems like finding a veil of obsession over the way I am looking today. Out of the blue, on my way, in black eyeliner, and amber red lipstick, I can't help but to feel so real within the pocket-length of my hovering sundress.

I slowly realize how beautifully I have outgrown those bullies of Srachi Das who used to criticize me for being brown and taller than most of the boys in my class, totally ignoring the fact that how she used to look like an ugly toad to me which I never cared to express. I remember the time in 10th grade, when she threw away my tiffin box just because I kept it in her place for a few moments for cleaning my desk as it got covered with chalk dust. I was hungry for half of the day and finally got to eat at 10 p.m after finishing off my boards' tuition class. Not only that, in 11th grade, she pushed me off from the second floor, kept me bleeding there all over my knees and elbows. She even came forward to see the damage and left the spot smiling when my eyes were bursting with tears from the fresh pain of uprooted flesh. Though Nikhil tried to put a complaint against her name, she saved herself by making it look like an accident with some soft drama and lies from the girls of her gang.

Later I got to know, she deeply hated me for being so close to Ishaan and when the rumor of our dating came out in the ground, she might have made a solid plan to maim me. Now, I see these people on social media, as the body positive influencers, teaching people to love their bodies and accept themselves after being a bully to others in all their lifetime.

By imagining them and comparing with my fragile self, suddenly the rudeness of the day felt lighter. Not only because I am a bit happier for other causes, but also remembering myself as a child-being kind to all my friends all the time, sharing tiffins even when my mom packed my favorite thing, and getting awarded extra marks for my soft and attentive behavior in class. Every morning I wake up, and choose to hate myself the most in the mirror, even in reality; those things are burdening me a little less today. And it's absolutely not because of the makeup and the dress-up I did for me, it's for the lenses I borrow from Adith to see myself through, in those different eyes, who admire mine.

"Mom, I am going out. I will buy a pizza back home. Thanks for letting me go. Bbye"- I shout from the dining hall while keeping the strides on.

"Do you take the papers and licenses, just in case…"- She comes into the hall and stops for a bit. "Wow, look, who's gonna steal the show today? Let me take a picture of you now. Wait!"- She runs to bring her phone and suddenly my existence starts feeling more valid.

"Mom…….I will be late. Leave me today"

"Shut up, it will take less than 5 minutes, stay there."- I hear the voice from her room with the creak of her wardrobe door which is pretty clear.

She came up with her phone and a paper flower from her wardrobe and made me pose in front of the wall painting, on which dad spent pretty well last year. After 20 minutes of photo session, I am finally allowed to go out with a deadline to maintain.

Reaching the front gate of the college, I see a bunch of happy faces jostling here and there. My windows arc closed as I keep the AC on to prevent both the humidity and the known faces away from me. I left a message when I was crossing the Ballygunge circular road, so, if I am not calculating it wrong, and he updated me with his correct time-run, he will be there in 2 more minutes. In between, I check my WhatsApp and find my mom has uploaded some of my pictures she took this morning, captioned, "Slaying college foundation day." Sometimes I feel how terribly backward I am from my own generation, where my mom is a thousand times ahead of it, nailing the trends under my nose, without shaping me into it.

I park the car in front of the fourth gate of the parking lot and send him the exact location to identify me easily. Seems like, my calculation wasn't wrong. He came in with busy feet, hopping over those small dividers with his long legs, and knocked at the closed window by my side.

It is a bright day, and the transient monsoon sun is pouring the light all over the rain-soaked streets, without making it warm enough to perspire. In a few days of rain for months, this is the only day rain smells like the fresh petals of mock orange-soothing and addictive to be inhaled frequently. It's not raining right now, but some pieces of the dark overcast aren't assuring the permanency of the feeble sun. I want it to rain today; a rain that can wash down all my qualms over the feelings I never expressed; a rain that can bring back my earnest self who isn't scared anymore to plunge into those delicate raindrops touching my skin.

I watch him coming in a blue full-sleeve sweatshirt; one sleeve is heaved to his elbow, probably to look at his wrist watch for catching time. The blue gets so much melted with his brightly fair complexion that I won't be surprised if it catches more nerves, including mine. Inside the view of my windshield glass, I watch his blue is slightly matching with the grave dark shade of the sky. He is looking like an oil painting, like the famous artists draw for their exhibition or any aesthetic portrait captured in an expensive camera. Once I thought to open my phone camera to blow the shutter and preserve these moments in my gallery, but it would be an embarrassment if he got any hint of capturing him without his permission. We aren't that close yet. So, I better prefer saving these for later, when I can actually fix him on my lock screen, and I don't have to ask for it.

"So, Kenny, where are you taking me today?"- He gets up in the car and sits beside me locking up the seatbelt after I point him to come in, over my closed window.

He is smelling nice but this is different from the first day. He changes the fragrances often and I wonder how amazingly they all dissolve in his skin like magic and make me wildly vulnerable, even though I try hard to stand against the fall.

"Ahhhh……I have thought about a place, but I need your confirmation first."

"Yeah?"- He squeezes his eyebrows at me.

"You heard about Belur Math?"

"Yah, sounds familiar. Maybe we can see some temples there. That's a famous place, but don't know the details very well."

"Very good. So, I am taking you there today. Trust me, you will feel the peace in your heart while coming back."

"I trust you. Let's go."

My heart splits up into pieces, like I am no longer my own. A part of me has already fallen into those words, and it feels like I am not being able to take myself back ever again. Don't know how he can phrase those million-dollar words so easily, like a whirr of wind. Trust is always harder than love, and I wasn't aware that I am actually capable of being trustworthy to someone I just met a few days back who doesn't even know how madly I am in love with him.

For one moment, I forget all the functions- where to go, what to do, how to drive forward; everything. But soon, I release myself back from his charms, take a deep breath, and hold onto the steering tighter. I don't know the roads very well, but as long as he is with me; I don't fear driving to the edge of the world. He's also a skilled driver, even better than me, so he can help me out if I am about to get run over by others.

I keep the maps on and start driving following the digital voice towards the unknown. The 8 p.m. deadline is still swirling on my head, but maybe it's too early to spoil the fun over it.

The further I go, I can see the darker to the darkest sky, spreading their friendly hands across the roads. I turn off the AC and open all the windows as the outer temperature may freeze us if I keep it on any longer. The sky is in its darkest shade of blue and the wind waves are most appropriate to be called sweeter than cooler. And when it touches my bare neck and hands, all my pores inhale the sensations of the blooming rain; I feel free and real, without any sugar coated happiness. This is the blue I crave for. I crave for this sky every day, to heal me inside out, all my bad times, my clumsiness, and all the dreams I kill every day.

These moments are priceless. With a momentary freedom to fly, a soulful steering in a grayer, breezy noon, and with the person of my whopping obsession- who would need something else to be happier? Perfection subsists. I have found it right here; between those clammy crossroads, over the crowded luxe cafes back and forth, and into the lusty existence of my El Amor. I wanna stick into these jiffies forever.

"Do you think it will start raining soon?"- I watch him introspecting the sky more often, and now he's looking for another assurance on his assumption. It's greyer and windy, so it can start raining any moment.

"Can we make it to the Belur math today? I ain't feeling very sure."- The next question comes without any gap. I feel that he's excited and anxious as we both can see that the chances of not reaching there are getting stronger with the drizzles.

After some time, the rain starts, like the forceful stream from a new shower knob, unbiased and intensely parallel with the sky. The raindrops on my front windscreen are falling down breaking into pieces like liquid crystals. The wiper blades are on heavy work but still the sight is blurry with cold steams and all I can see is an unclear view of my darling city clustered with the cars of those who also have made a bad choice of planning a trip on a rainy afternoon and now surviving on the busy hands of their wiper blades just like us. Earlier on this road, the view was clear enough to look at the farthest traffic signals easily, but suddenly rain made life slower and blurry, where there are vehicles all around me. That's the time I start feeling a little scared. My inefficient hands on the steering aren't that steady in slippery roads, and with the little distances between it's not very impossible to get tripped by, and make a collision.

When the cars start moving slowly, I feel a rigid grip on my hand pushing the gear into the first one. Among all the fear and hassle, I totally forgot that I was in third gear, and to the depth I pushed the accelerator, which would definitely make a hit while thinking about it. Adith somehow noticed it on time and saved both of our asses from a severe mishap.

"You aren't here, are you?"- He seems a bit frustrated.

"I am so sorry; I am not very efficient on damp roads. I just…………… got scared. Am sorry, am so sorry."

I may convince him a bit, but he opens the door, slams it shut, comes to my side and makes his hand forward to hold mine.

"Come on, switch the sides. We are going back home. I don't think the rain is gonna stop any sooner. Save the place for a sunny day. We will definitely go there. For now, you need a break."

The absurd dominance in his voice subdues my so-called 'superiority'. I look at him like an aimless fool, as if my face of innocence can make him go back and let me sit there for a while. The appeals in his face are unavoidable and somehow, he's absolutely right about me. I need a break or maybe I want a sight of him, driving my car and taking me to the infinite. For now, the infinite is home.

I held his hand and his touch made my soul on fire. A single flash of lightning played across my skin and in those chilly winds, I started getting little droplets of sweat huddled in my forehead. His grip is strong, manly and a little bit harsh probably due to intense workout, and his one pull made me up from the seat and got me out of the frame.

I go back to his place and feel the warmth he made there for me. Being on his seat feels like being on top of him, like a cuddle, and that is all I am craving for now, this rainy afternoon.

"There's chocolate inside the cupboard. You can have it if you want. I brought some nachos too. In case, you feel hungry."- I don't know if this is not a definition of *perfect*, then what else it is, and how my messy life manages to come across with someone just the way I always wanted. Not even my brother ever offers me this much care and comfort, and within a month he made me feel like home.

"Aren't you hungry?"- He watches me watching him for a long time, and his sexy smirk amplifies that he gets me totally the way I didn't.

"I do. You want one?"

"Sure. I am terribly hungry. If you would have planned a little late, I surely would have cooked something for yah. But didn't get enough time to do the shopping and cooking."

"Holy crap! You cook too? Make me something someday. I would love to taste that."- I break the chocolate bar in the middle and use my teeth to tear up the nachos packet and place it in the bottle holder. Dad made this space on the very first day we bought the car, for keeping all the foods and drinks at a handy distance to run his mouth while driving. Didn't know it would come to use one day.

"Come over to my place anytime. I will make you some."

"Won't your landlord take you amiss for bringing girls there?"

"We are just friends, c'mon! Why can't I bring you in? Just let me know when you are coming."

I lower my eyes from his face. He is right. We are just friends and I shouldn't be making things complicated by imagining him from my bottom to my bed. He craved for a friend, not the things I am trying to slide into his brain. So, I should make a halt here and go back where we started.

"Tomorrow, is it okay for you? If you can manage the morning, I can drive you back home."

I watch how his face doesn't make any change while offering me those words. Maybe it was just a mirage, and only I was falling for us. From his side, I am just an insecured, lonely soul who can't be anything but a friend.

"Tomorrow is a holiday after today's celebration. So, my mom won't allow me to…"- I press the smile between my thin lips to look guiltily formal. I wish I could leave the place in a huff and let him realize I don't appreciate the idea of being friends, but that is never a choice.

"The day after tomorrow? I know you love brownies; I will make one for you. And how about pasta? Mac?"

I don't know how he is naming my favorite dishes one after another when we hardly had any conversation over it. Maybe I should go, to keep his *friendly* invitation and come back home being insomniac for a whole week. It's him, his presence that turns me on like a drug, and I shouldn't be judgmental if he doesn't feel the same way.

"That sounds good. Will text you the time."

He stops the car at a sleep-walking distance from my house. From there, I take the charge towards the garage and he leaves for his cab standing on the nearby road, after waving me *'bye'*.

My deadline was 8'o' clock at night, and it's just 4:30 in the afternoon, but the solemnity of the clouds makes it look like a dusky midnight. I entered the dining room and saw mom putting all the attention together on the TV screen. It is her favorite serial, so I need to call her up.

"Mom, I am home, and I am hungry."

She lifts her face up, and I notice the waving wonders, drifting across it.

"It's afternoon, Kenny? What? Nobody let you be in their game? I don't know why you have become so unsocial?"

Mom gets up and steps towards the kitchen.

"Mom, I am in college now, and there's no game. I am hungry and I need food, right nowwwww."

I yell like a crass and my tone is so rude that I even start judging myself after I finish the sentence. Today was supposed to be my best day so far. It started like a dream, but I absolutely hate the idea of being friends. Nikhil is my friend, the boy who helped me complete my project last year was my friend, the boy in my drawing class who used to save a seat for me was my friend; but how the hell on earth I made him think I want friendship from these unnamed interests. I want him as the rivers want the cascades, as the sky wants the sun, as a drowning man wants the strand. He is as precious as a breath to me. I built hopes around him every single day, and all he did was play me like a single blow that crushed my castle of cards into dirt.

"You had a bad day, and I have nothing to do with that. Don't you try to put your anger on me just because you were silent in front of those who caused it! Go upstairs and freshen up. It will be ready till then."

I admire how incredibly right she is about my broken emotions. I should speak up to Adith and tell him that I never want him as a friend. Maybe it would end today, but at least I wouldn't be in this swirling entanglement. I wish I did it, and freed myself from all those sleepless nights of open-eyed dreaming. I wish I was brave enough to walk away from situations like this, love myself a little more when someone else refused to do that for me. I wish everything was as easy as I wanted it to be!

OUR MAGIC

I got Nikhil's text when I was curling up my lashes to get ready for Adith's house. Even though he tagged "Just friends" in my intention, that was never enough to put out the fire he kindled in my heart. I was still gonna love him as intensely as before, but in this case, he was never going to know that.

"I am not coming tomorrow. Got caught up by the seniors and have to stay here for our Fresher's. So, you have to go to the library by yourself. I will be there next weekend."

Nikhil and I go to the library most weekends and spend hours cooping up our heads inside those piles of books and sometimes sleep there until the bookkeeper reminds us to leave. We both love reading different genres and for us it's the best way to keep a peaceful friendship and staying away from fighting over silly reasons.

Nikhil mostly picks sci-fi, high school-drama, horror fiction, thriller and others. For me mystery, romance, war histories, fiction and sometimes non-fiction do the work. We have been members in this library since we were 12 and those abrupt rides from comics to adult fiction haven't made us any less thrilled than we used to be before. We still get thrilled if it's a new release and sometimes put our heads together in one book so one doesn't have to stress the taste with an abominable spoiler.

To be very honest, in those troubling thoughts of accepting or forbidding Adith's invitation, I totally forgot about the library morns and its last-minute quick fix. So, if Nikhil wouldn't cancel it, I was probably gonna remember it the next day while he was waiting for me at the door. He didn't know about Adith yet, and the moments we shared as *friends*. I should have texted him about those rides, but found out those were nothing but some very normal friendly-activities, in a bit of early baking. The scattered pieces of puzzles were still indicating his adolescence over me. Even after taking hours to think if there were any special words or efforts from him that would make it look like more than just a friendship, I didn't find any. Maybe adult age friendships are like making your friend feel special or gifting her the most thoughtful things; else he wouldn't name it *friendship* after making me sneaking around my house at midnight and dragging me down to the lake to see the stars or comforting me after my stupid mistake and drive me home safely with a generous warmth.

"It's okay. Send me those fresher's videos whenever you get it."

There came a "Hmmm" in reply, which has been normalized between friends, else it's a sign of ignorance or an unwillingness to talk further without any doubt.

I bagged the snacks I bought for him as he didn't have a sweet tooth, and stepped towards the cab waiting outside for me. My mom was a bit confused seeing me taking a cab for college as I never spent this much while traveling somewhere I don't like. Therefore I said her bye and I didn't see any wrinkles of doubt in her face. The way I failed to socialize myself to the outer world and became homesick in the age of becoming the opposite, it's unfair to have doubts on my reliability. Maybe she couldn't even think of me seeing someone and trying hard not to be in love with him. This brutal age was changing me and so far the changes weren't so great.

I reached his house at 12:30 and called him from the outside of the main gate. It was a huge house and of course huge enough for two people. His landlord, Mr. Sen was a lonely old man with no relatives and neighbors around. He never cared to get married, and now in his 60's, he is batting alone like AB De Villiers.

Adith came down within a few moments after getting my call, and accompanied me to the garden where Mr. Sen was watering those freshly cut and dewormed leaves. First I thought he would send me home after reading my face, guilty enough for hiding feelings which were already overwhelming from my eyes. But he scrutinized me for a while from the little gap of his glasses, sticking a bit down from where they were supposed to be, and asked, "Your name?"

"Kiyana……Kiyana Mukherjee."

The fear of judgments already made my face pale as Monday mornings, and his glance of cold eyes baffled me to talk further. Seeing that, Adith took the charge from there.

"She is my friend. I invited her for lunch. Would you mind if we munch in my room till the evening?"

He didn't say anything. He just went away to do what he was doing before. Adith waved me in and we both went to his room crossing the staircase and a big hallway with organized and neatly cleaned furniture. To see that small part of the house, I had to admit that Mr.Sen was very passionate about the things he possessed and his admiration towards maintaining the house is rare in this apartment-culture.

We reached his room and suddenly my room started seeming like a rat-hole to me. Kanishk's room was bigger than mine, but compared to Adith's, it was nothing. His one room consists of a big couch to lie on, binge movies and an open kitchen just a hand's distance from the couch, with properly equipped cooking environment, and at the end of the huge kitchen-dining room, there was his bedroom with an attached bathroom. He even had the bedroom corner reserved as the working section with a table and an ergonomic mesh chair. He had the perfect room that my 14-year-old-self had ever wished for. Gradually the wishlist got bigger as I grew up, but reality betrayed me pretty well. So, if I got that place as mine, I would never interact with the external world; intentionally!

He told me to make myself comfortable and change those outside clothes if I was carrying any extra. But the thing was I never thought of changing clothes at his place as it was just a lunch invitation just like my relatives' and also I didn't think myself of being that comfortable in our first house-visit. So, he lent me one of his shorts which was pretty big for me and smiled when I was looking even skinnier in those baggy fits.

When I reached his place, he was left with some last minute items, so now, he came back to the kitchen to finish the cooking while I was placing those snacks on his dining table, each of which I bought from different departmental stores after Googling their best snacks available.

Soon I got bored hearing him stirring those mesh skimmers and laid down on the couch facing my legs to the window.

"You must be bored. Let me get you some books. Would you like something to drink?"

"You don't need to be busy with me. I can pass hours staring at the window."

He smiled and came back with two drinks after a while- a cranberry coffee for me and a chilled beer for him. He put off the apron at a side of his kitchen slab, stretched his legs to the lower square of his center table and looked at me with a soft smile, leaning his head on the edge of the couch.

"You are tired. I troubled you a lot. Didn't I?"- I said, squeezing my eyes with a smile.

"If this is a trouble, I would love to have this every day."- His face brightened with a smile.

I didn't know what he actually tried to mean, but it definitely felt like hope. In between, my clumsy hands spilled the coffee over my t-shirt and as it was a V-neck cut, some drops of it entered even deeper that needed a closed door to wipe off.

"Wait up, let me bring a piece of cloth."

I was so embarrassed that I forgot to get up and reach the sink to wash my hands and pat it dry afterwards. I sat emptily until he brought a towel to dry me and then hand it over to me for cleaning those coffee stains. I finally placed the glass on the table and cleared my neck area as far I could reach without lowering my t-shirt. But inside, it was wet and unless I blew it dry, my innerwear was sculpting its presence from the damp spot.

Adith looked at it once and turned his eyes upwards to mine. There was a small sigh of discomfiture when I caught him staring at my breasts, with a glance as steady as a piston of an engine. I could've smiled a little to neutralize his guilt, but I didn't. My eyes possessed interrogation, austere judgments, as rigid as hell, like I didn't want him to stare. But I did, I wanted him to look at me, to touch me like hell, to feel me from inside out and the curves, his stupid had coffee created.

The face of embarrassment didn't go away. He sucked his breathes to say, "You can wear my t-shirt, if it's not a problem. I will dry your clothes quickly. It will take ten to twenty minutes."

I nodded and let him go inside to bring his t-shirt. He came up with a lounge t-shirt which looked twice of my size. He was a lean and muscular guy, who loved to wear baggy clothes at home, so all his house t-shirts were of same fit for me. He gave me ample options, but all of them were so manly that I couldn't find any to catch my eye. Heading towards the couch, he chose a grey round-neck t-shirt among all the pieces that were lying over it. I took it to his bedroom and locked it up from inside. First few minutes, I rolled my eyes all over his bedroom, and finally started admiring the efforts he put into making it look perfectly neat and clean. His bed-facing mirror was huge and the big half-circle case underneath, was holding all his male maquillage. The case was marvel-made and his fragrances and other things were lying there in an unorganized way. I was right about him from the first day. He used different French colognes on every meet, none of which was available in India.

He had a wooden comb and a shaving box from a luxury brand, lying over the marvel slab and all these cleaning accessories and branded smells unveiled the mystery of the heavenly fragrances lingering in my nose from the moment I entered into his bedroom.

Therefore I pulled off my t-shirt and looked into the mirror to see how far the coffee stains made it through. Some of the droplets rolled down straight and stopped just upon my navel. In all those days, I actually saw myself this close for the very first time. During all those times of coming back home, throwing my t-shirts on bed and putting on a new one, never made me stop and stare at my body which I built with all those regular-stretches and some morning workout routines. I used to hate mirrors and cameras in high school as my self-esteem had been shortened by the brown complexion I possess among all those white-toned kids. I used to fake excuses in every school function, and successfully eluded all those group pictures our teachers forced us to click. Nobody can ever find my face on the graduation board, rather they would find my writing in the school magazine, probably something that had made them think. I wrote about the world, its people, their emotions and a hunt towards its annihilation. Everyone read about it, but nobody dug into it. So, to be precise, they all know me, but they don't really know me.

But here, probably for the first time in my life, I saw myself this generously without those clothes. Suddenly, all my complaints knocked over and I started admiring how amazingly toned I was away from the layers of extra fleshes that eventually pile up around your lower abs due to bad eating habits and sometimes for the genes you carry. The enormous years of being criticized as a toothpick, I felt blessed for being that. Chubby is beautiful as long as you are celebrating the beauty of those who are wishing to accept themselves as amazing as they already are. And from those high school years, I gained much more weight that actually forced me to start working out to stay in shape. Standing in front of the mirror, I was thanking myself for sticking into a healthy routine which was not very easy and exciting to stick to.

I was in my bra and denim and trying to figure out if those coffee drops could've made me any sexier. My eye liner was intact and his dreamy mirror-light made me stare even more into it. I moved my face towards the mirror to look into my eyes as the way Adith looked into me, tried to imagine him feeling my shoulders from behind. I wondered how he found me beautiful at a glance when I was struggling hard to love myself in all these cruel years.

My bra was wet, so was my chest and even if I took off my t-shirt and wore his, I would catch a cold by soaking the liquid from the bra pads to my skin. While watching me over and over in the mirror light, I didn't notice that the lock got opened due to my loose grip. So, After a few moments, Adith walked in, unhesitatingly as the door was opened and saw me rubbing my left clavicle as the coffee stain was easier to shove off in that part.

We both were shocked seeing each other at a wrong moment, and neither of us was prepared enough to react to a situation like that. He stopped like a bronze statue, fixing his eyes on mine as if he was scared to lower it. A t-shirt was hanging from his elbow and his other hand was holding the door knob. I couldn't move my eyes from him either, but somehow managed to cross my hands over my chest, shielding it over from those lusty stares.

It seemed like he was glued in that pose and waiting for me to speak up. So, I did.

"I am not done yet."- My hands were still across my chest with just a tighter shield.

"I am so sorry. The door was open, so I thought I should offer…... It may be a little less baggy for you."- He spoke finally.

I didn't say a word and saw him closing the door and begged his pardon again. I stood there still for some moments, and suddenly some witty thoughts conquered my nerves. I called him in. And when he came, I kissed on his bearded cheeks. Till today, I don't know why I did what I did, but nothing like that crossed my mind ever again. I was desperate to touch him and to be touched back. The longing I grew in my heart eventually came to a melting point. Seeing him that day, in my purview, my holy hormones tore down the flexes. I was no longer the girl scratching papers and crumpling it up over the dustbin to take control of the emotions crossing their boundaries. I was a woman for the moment- a woman with needs, big enough to fly high and forget all those eyes of criticism that had been made a social taboo.

He looked at me - shocked, delicate, needy and fucked up like I seeded a lust with one kiss. I saw him fisting his hand and drawing his legs two steps back to hold the marvel case as a support. I was still in the same attire as he saw me the latest and his eyes were flicking from my head to toe by several rounds.

Within a few moments, he came closer, pulled my back against the wall, straightened my hand lining around his waist and smudged a kiss. I was never been kissed before on my lips. He broke my lip-virginity, along with this the restraints I drew for myself. It was just a kiss, a sober one but that feeling too, created a pandemonium in my heart. It was the first kiss of my life. Additionally, it was from my favorite mouth I wanted to touch so bad! But those moments stayed no longer. He looked at me once with a lusty smile and dove into a deeper side, with me.

The movements of his hands weren't sure. It was hovering over every place he could reach with the utmost formality. I can't say he crossed the line, but if he did, it would be a bit more relishing.

I was of course a bad kisser, and in the bustle of his small bites, my other senses were ingurgitating his smell- the same French cologne in a different way.

We took a break in the middle and I finally got a chance to free my lips to talk.

"Aren't we just friends? Friends don't do this."

"Not anymore."- His face lit up with a grin, a hungry stare, dripping with lust, and some soulful cravings trying to hide underneath. I coveted his smile, and we started again.

In between those forbidden hours of kissing, his microwave oven tuned in after completing the baking. We stopped for a while, and he looked at me with a glare of queries. I knew what was the actual need of me there - a nod, to confirm him flowing on me. I didn't say anything, neither did I give any nod, but his stare didn't leave me aside and I swear I didn't have any power to turn my eyes down. His eyes had a magic - like the magic new leaves bring to the earth, looking for a respite of new hopes. If his kisses were riddles, his stare held the spell. Those spells were of the magic, Our Magic - extremely selfish and delicately stimulating.

My eyes were on him with a glittering smile in it. It was engulfing his face like the most luscious ellipse I never wanted to get over. I didn't know where to stop, when to stop and why to stop, since no better way would excite me more.

He put his hand on my left shoulder, slowly brought it in to my ears and plugged all those messy hair right behind it. His fingertips were full of care. A single touch and I was almost halfway dead. I shrouded my arms across his waist and pulled myself close enough so that his nose could touch my chin. He sighed a long breath, looked like pondering a vast world of confusions.

"Quit looking at me like you want me so bad. The hell I know, you don't, you won't ever."- He faltered.

All these time, I only thought I wanted him so bad and never tried to figure out how it would look if it happens from the other side. From the outer crust of his intellectual prowess, I somehow forgot to unfold the reality inside. Maybe he had a soft heart who just wanted much more than my freaky admirations. Maybe he wanted something from me, something I was capable of giving, something that I could never get short of. You never know until you sue the mantle and successively reach the core.

"I am hungry."- I had so much to tell, to free him from the speculation he thrived in his mind, but all that was so much, that it could exhaust the day off and ruin my side if a slightest of him got me wrong. So, I change the words, off topic, to elude the hardest part temporarily. That was definitely not the right time to express my craziness over him. It could easily be misleading as a lust-talking, and there was a chance he might name it as immaturity. He was still in my arms and I didn't want to let go of the feeling.

Also I was starving from the moment he brought me the coffee. I couldn't say due to being questioned over the feminine regime like it's strictly prohibited for women to eat freely on the first date.

I can say, it was our official first date as he named the previous ones as friendly outings, and he never wanted me to see this side of him before.

"Sure"

He moved his eyes off from me and turned back towards his kitchen. I didn't know what he was feeling, but my heart was dying with all those inextricable words I buried behind the bars. My mind was a mess. Neither I could read him properly, nor was I trying to let him read mine. Intimacy doesn't bring love every time. Sometimes it clatters with the soft dust that you fermented on your inhumanity. For me, all those years of dejection and those infused hatred; I forget to be human again. I wanted to be free, like I could easily cry for help when I was a child, or to fist the shirt sleeves of my dad in fear of being left alone in the street crowd, like I could punch Kanishk knowing he wouldn't punch me back even if it made him bleed. In these years of puberty, the thing I learnt the most is to be silent; silent until my existence does weigh enough. Till then my pain, my feelings are meaningless, as imprudent as the existence of the moon in the daylight. Not everything in it was wrong, but it was way too much and nothing at the same time.

Adith made a huge dining which could easily be called as a small feast, mac and cheese with sourdough bread, fried chicken for starters and the smokey brownie with a butterscotch scoop for dessert. To be very honest, after those flaming kisses, everything looked lesser as a serving. To be with him, itself was a treat and none of his food could be as delicious as him.

I wore his baggy tee and came to the table after he was done with the decoration.

"You start eating, I have to rush to Mr. Sen and then I am joining in. It's already late as a lunch."

"Can I go?"- I said cause I found nothing unlikely.

Adith took a few seconds to think if it would be a great idea or not, then he confirmed, "Let's go."

Crossing the staircase, and the front face of the balcony, we knocked at his door and the first thing he saw opening it was my face, my poor hesitant face. Adith went inside in silent feet and I saw him organizing those pots on his kitchen table and went back to wash off his hands after he was done. He was a boy of bewitchment and anyone who had seen me seeing him the way I used to stare at his every step, could easily pretend the madness I bred inside me. Mr. Sen was an experienced man. He crossed all the tarns and stones of aging like an old owl. My feelings couldn't elude his wise eyes and I got it pretty clearly when he said, "I won't say 'no' to you, but no longer than 5 p.m. And try to be silent when you come over. I am not familiar with noisy footsteps in my house."

I nodded and my cheeks got cherry-red as the colors of modesty. Adith heard it all, but acted like he didn't and we both went upstairs maintaining the awkwardness of silence. Even after sitting at the dining table, the awkwardness wasn't about to ease. Questions caged up inside, scared to knock at the door. What we did before would be perfectly normal if we both accepted the feelings without making things uncomfortable. But, I was still looking for multiple cases of what he said.

Why does he even think that I don't want him the way I show, when what I show is not even enough compared to what is thriving inside me!

"Adith, should we do this again?"- I asked while taking a spoonful in my mouth. I should say he had a perfect hand in cooking. The brownie and pasta melted my heart faster than it was supposed to melt in my mouth, perfect food from my perfect guy.

"Only if you want it."- I knew this smirk, a smirk of equivocation. It was a trap to test me if I really could confess or not. He wanted me to say it.

"Do you want me to come again?"- I wanted to say too, but I just got out of the line.

"From now on, it's your place too. Wish to dive in anytime you want. If I had the choice, I would rather keep you right here than letting you come and go, but looks like it's never an option."

His words made my soul dance a little. This was the first time he told me that he wanted me without any second opinion. He wanted me to stay there with him, to watch him all day, to snuggle, to do something more, behind closed doors. And for him, I wanted the same, to touch him without any occasion, to see him surviving his day like a normal person doing the dishes, washing clothes, dusting, cooking, and hitting the couch at the end of the day with those sleep-soaked eyes.

"I can come here over from college. My classes are pretty early now. So, I can buzz you up, after it's done."

"Sounds like a plan. I can manage to keep you after 5, if you are comfortable slipping through the window."

"What!!!!!!"

"Yah"- His laugh sounded like an assurance. "I do it all the time. What do you think? I went to your alley in the middle of the night and my landlord opened the door for me? He's friendly but strict. So, my windows are the only options when I feel suffocated at home. You should try it once."

Really! Escaping from the window! It was big enough to fit me though, but I never go downstairs even when I am dying of thirst, and wait in my room lying dry until my mom rushes me some new water bottles and takes the old ones for refill. I am the queen of idles, and jumping out of a window isn't absolutely my thing. What if I hit the ground in my bones and break one to never jump properly again! What if Mr. Sen catches me up and calls my parents for sneaking into his house in those forbidden hours. This is insane.

"I will obviously try it out, that will be fun."

P.S. Don't fall in love. It will make you do crazy things.

L'AMOUR

To reach his house, I had to take the metro and a long walk afterwards until I got the view of his balcony, perfectly fixed with the colorful flower tubs. These days the roads seem much more meaningful than they ever did. My college was also on the same route, but it never made me feel like enjoying the streets, its people, and those tempting lights according to the lyrics my earphones were infusing in my head.

I never thought the route I hated the most would bring me this much happiness one day. But I couldn't lie all the time. Some days I had to attend some early classes so that I could run to him with much time in my hand, and some days I didn't attend at all. We cuddled, kissed, slept on each other, he cooked, I watched, and some days he just hunted my college notebooks for any interesting chapter to study. He was a CA under weekend training in an audit firm, the place that used to make him forget about the world he had other than his upcoming profession, the place that stole him for living those hours of dedication without letting me be a part of it. So, other than the weekends, he was at home, and he was all mine.

His bedroom had an attached, movable bookshelf, as huge as the doors of the ancient Mughal palaces, loaded with accounting, auditing and other books that I didn't have any idea about. Apart from that, his grip on programming languages was remarkable.

Even my projects stopped asking for Nikhil's help as he was fulfilling me to the brim in everything.

Taking the off-route to the common way, I started thinking if I should attend the first class or I should go to his house directly. Batu Onat was on my shuffle and I got stuck on his "Impatient", especially on a line where he addressed his lover's wildness as an incompatible desire to his love for slowing things down.

Along with the orchestration, those lines were awakening my senses to paint him with my own idea of intimacy just like a rock star on spotlight; unsolvable and delirious. Our kisses were pure, not wild. If it were, it wouldn't stop only in kisses. It would definitely cross the boundary of being dressed in a place where no third pair of eyes was rolling for adjudication, invading our privacy.

The day seemed too witty to waste over listening to the professor and the boring OS lectures in her typical rural accent I hated. I had a toxic relationship with my college and a big part of it was that they never made me fall in love with it. I never thought that I didn't fit in there, rather than it's more likely that they never fitted into mine. The way I grew up and the way I had witnessed my brother's college life, mine seemed like a vengeance of the two precious school-final years I wasted on people like Ishaan. Maybe I deserved it pretty badly. The resentment came with the heaviness of my heart. I was partially responsible for the hell I was offered to serve for those three fucking years, with no friends, no good teacher, no fun, no real learning and of course no life.

While turning back to close the gate latch, I felt a slow-feet coming towards me scrunching the dry leaves. It was the end of monsoon, so the sky stopped being a nagging child and pouring all the time.

I looked around and saw Mr.Sen with a big watering can, treading all over his garden and not even cared to greet me once. I absolutely love when someone doesn't try to fit into the glaze knowing there would be nothing but awkwardness. I am not a very social person, and neither I am one of those who keep switching apps in order to escape loneliness. Solitude is an embracing vector of my life. The more time I get alone, the more I try to learn about myself. It's a never-ending lesson of what I start loving in a new frame and what I am no longer afraid of losing. Some people just can't cop up with the idea of being alone. For them, even the infinite internet contents aren't enough to stop feeling like it.

I opened the front gate of his house as silently as possible and heard Mr.Sen finally speak up, "5 p.m. shouldn't be 5:01.". When I looked back, I didn't see him turning to my face. He was still caring his plants, watering them and plucking the rotten leaves in between. It was just a reminder to put in my head that he wanted me to vanish before the sun went down.

While I was unwinding my shoe laces, I saw Adith coming down in lazy feet. His eyes; soaked in comfort, boxers pushed a little upward, and his face held an admirable smile. He probably heard his landlord or the squeak of the front gate and guessed me walking over; else his nappy face wouldn't be visible coming downstairs for a confirmation.

"Hey, you are early today."- His mouthful of smile warmed my heart. At least he was happy seeing me a bit early on the clock.

I smiled, keeping my eyes down.

He took me to his room, locked the door in busy hands, pressed me against it and emerged into a deep kiss, genuinely what's called a smooch. I was tucking my hands inside his t-shirt, trying to touch his bare skin with my slightly moist fingertips. The suddenness of his kisses made me sweat a little.

He was sensitive, thirsty and warm; as warm as the desperate sun rays on a winter morning. His smooches were wild, breaking the improper barriers of innocence. We were young; we were supposed to be wild and this was the first phase of feeling it. His hands were approaching upwards, but he stopped before going mainstream.

"Is it okay? Will you be……"

"Don't ask, do it."- I didn't let him finish.

I threw my bag on the couch, and we both rushed to the bedroom. He went up on the bed first and leaned against the headboard slat. Then he swung me up on his lap and we started it again. Now, his hands took off my shirt first, but stuck at the hooks, roughly making a great trouble to workout at that high time. Then he figured out somehow and stopped before taking it off, "Can I?"

"Yes."- My '*Yes*' was so seducing that it splintered all my hesitations open. He seemed to get a boost after me and that made the foreplay amazing.

After a while, our hormones even drove crazier. We were crossing the threshold and I already felt him getting harder by time. He was lying on me and his hands were inside my bottoms, bringing the flood of happy hormones in me altogether. I was so high that I almost forgot there was something else ahead of it. A sex, a proper sex as the absolute firth of two bodies.

"Would you like to proceed?"- The sex-talking was getting more intense.

"Yes, do it."

"Are you sure? You said it would be your first time!"

"Yes. That's why I want you to be my first, probably the last too."

"Is it real? You are too beautiful to be true. I don't know if I am capable enough to take care of you properly. I will proceed only if you are ready. Else we can do it another day whenever you feel like doing it."

"I am ready, you dummy. And stop being a saint in bed. I love you and haven't stopped loving you from the very day we met. How explicitly do you want me to say it now? Be on my knees and cry it to hear you can't love me back! I am tired of being in this drama. I don't want to be your friend, I want……."

He kissed me to stop proceeding further as if he already knew it before. His touch felt safe, like a refugee. My eyes were damp in the fulfillment of the freaky reality that was somehow coinciding my ideas of him, I sketched every night. His desires were contagious and those lips were sometimes respiting from mine, to reach my forehead and drawing kisses there to heal. I closed my eyes to feel his breath all over my body. He slowly removed my bottoms, then briefs and started with his fingers. When I opened my eyes, I saw him taking off his pants, wearing the rubber wear, and thrusting his hardness into my numb soft. His face was at a contagious distance to my mouth, graved into my left clavicles straight on his jaw. His heavy breathing not only made my excitements touch the roof; it also braced my pains into a knot of desires where I was too horny to get scared.

My body was getting heavier in an unknown fear and the severe pain of physically stepping into adulthood grasped my nerves. At some point of time, I thought I should cry him to stop, but the far I read in those online articles, I knew that the first times are always painful. But he stopped there without waiting for me to cry. Maybe he saw it in my face.

"Are you okay? Your face has become red."

"I am alright."

"You don't look alright. We should stop here. Is it hurting you badly?"

"It is paining, but I think I can take it once."

"You know, you can say *no*, if you want to."

"I know. We are good enough."

"Words to my lady."

And he started again. I closed my eyes and clattered my teeth together as a spate of blood came out of me unconventionally. The pain was crumpling my stomach and I could no longer hold back my tears, seeing all the fluids of my body came on a strike in sum, leaving me high and dry inside out.

He stopped right there and readily cleared the blood and the stain. He dressed me up, took me back to bed after changing the bed sheet and did all the cleaning. He also wrapped up my lower belly in a warm towel and it actually worked to alleviate the pain.

For an hour, we couldn't talk a word and all I could hear was his fastening heartbeat as he was holding me closer enough to huddle over his heart. His lips were on my forehead, kissing frequently as it was the only expression left to the end. I felt his breaths were dispersing on my face, cared not to interrupt my sleep when I found myself been stared at after a power nap. His face was full of purity and gracefulness, the face of that day on the very moment - I can't ever forget.

"Are you tired? Do you need a coffee?"- He asked while tucking my hair behind my ears with his fingertips. His gaze was straight into me, firm, assertive and full of life, not even catching a glimpse too often.

"Is it already 5?"- My voice was creeping in laziness.

"It's only 1. I can keep you here for a few more hours."

We both slept half-naked under the blanket, upper body kept bare to melt into one. The thermostat was on 18, so it was biting the skin without a blanket. The cold was comforting not only because the lazy hours are incomplete without dry air, but it also brings the warmth together for a better time spent. In that ambiance, his body felt like reaching the shore after a stormy night, a halt with peace and a strong hope for getting back home. He was my home, a strong feeling of him. The smell of his skin was magnetic, the *cheiro no cangote*, French perfume on his sweat - blinding my sensations, mending me on the other way. This feeling was heaven- his nuzzle on my neck, holding him closer, feeling him inside, crafting some unnamed letter on his naked chest. The search was over. The longing for someone I was meant to be with, was over. I found him, and I wasn't escaping from that feeling.

THE SUN AND THE STORM

I always prefer Friday sunsets over Sunday mornings, especially when it's the pitfall of winter. The satisfaction of knowing two whole-hearted days of freedom and late mornings under warm blanket is more enjoyable than the days spent themselves. Winter never actually loved my city that much. It left in more ways than it found reasons to stay. When the north and mid India is rattling teeth by the cold crunches in the downfall of soft temperature, our sun makes us put off the mufflers when the clock hits 12 midday. Winter is never arousing here. It's often comfortable and more like a picnic season in Kolkata unless it starts raining. But being the one who always admires rain in every season, I never find it irritating like daily wagers. Their point is stronger than my thirst of seeing the raindrops on my glass window; but the heart wants what it wants.

Fridays were more fun because Nikhil used to be back home and we used to spend Saturday morns playing Spiderman or watching cartoons together and save our energy for a long day in the library. But as the time got older with us, his attachment to his college took over our weekend schedules. If the reasons were limited in his college life, it would be less concerning for me. But he got a girlfriend there. So, mostly he was hooking up with a teacher from a different department - older, dominant, and apparently heavy on his nerves, when I was trying to figure things out all by myself.

My Insecurities wouldn't thrive if he would just be the 'Nikhil' I knew. But he had changed. His priorities had changed. My texts no longer found him responsive. He stopped coming back home on weekends, and didn't care to let me know about it. I hardly received any text from him and whenever I called, either there was a busy IVR tone or he let it ring without a potential call back. When I told him about my incidents with Adith, he was indifferent; didn't take much interest to react. "Good for you."- It was his only reply. And when I asked the reason of his impassivity, he told that he was so much in love with that teacher that he couldn't miss a chance of meeting her at the weekends, so he was abandoning our weekend plans and his family for romanticizing that woman for some lonely time he got, away from his crazy college pals.

I was not against his relationship until it nudged me in the fear of losing my best friend. It's not that we talked every day for hours or I couldn't breathe without letting him know about everything in my day, but when something happens, I still choose Nikhil to speak first rather than anybody else. He was my ultimate solver, and to a certain point, I vividly felt like I was losing the bonding. Maybe my love was way too much that even the slightest change in him made me lose my world. My friendship was intense, unlike him, so, moving on from the brotherly memories wasn't that easy that he made it look like.

On weekdays, I was mostly in Adith's house - dancing, laughing, reading, cuddling, having sex, or sleeping on his chest until it was the time to come back. So, weekdays really weren't that prominent as the weekends.

After a course of time, Nikhil started getting vanished from my recent logs. I stopped calling him and he never cared enough to check in. To be very honest, when the anger and jealousy summoned me together, I refused to make room for it. But my weekends were pathetic, jagged crack with the memories and left overs. Adith had busy weekends, so I couldn't call him either. Rather than spending time with mom and accompanying her watching those boring serials, the only thing left was to find the library enjoyable alone. For the first few weeks, it was an anguish, left alone to heal. But later, I felt it no more when I forced myself to face the facts. Whatever was done, came from his side. He ended the friendship and probably became happier when my texts no longer stuck in the pile of his unseen notifications. Letting go is the art I learnt from an early age. Possession was never my thing. I accepted the fact that I was always a luxury in everyone's life, never could become the need. So, when it's the high time, I am easily revoked without any second thought. They just enjoyed my presence; they never needed me.

Some days I sat in his seat and try out a new genre that he could've picked if he was there. It was very weird of me that I stopped missing the fights over the same book and started enjoying the serenity it brought me when left alone. The librarian used to stop sometimes and lower his specs to ask if my friend was doing okay, but soon Saturdays got familiar with Nikhil's absence, and it no longer felt hard to take the long route alone while returning home.

The Monday morning of 2nd December was special. It was Adith's birthday. I was more excited to make it a birthday-like birthday with a day of celebration when we could shut our world for others. Even though I stayed up a lot with him lately, he was not a typical guy glued to his girlfriend all the time. Most of the time, he used to be busy doing his things. He told me once that he got a few of his own clients while working in that office and they pretty much liked his work. And from them, more clients were making it to him and it never happened that we got a single peaceful hour without his phone ringing. Some days he used to give me a paperful of sums and counted on my footsteps in case I was trying to escape those. Later he came back and unfolded all the knots that kept being unrealistic to me. His intelligence was seductive. It burned me every time like an unknown fire that never came at an ease.

Spending time with him never meant we were always on our hormones. I don't know why his new clients, his seniors, and his mates never hesitated to call him without any time sense. He was mostly studying, taking phone calls, cooking, or sometimes scrutinizing my college lessons to keep my hands off from stalking his every move unswervingly. He was a book addict, and seeing him drowning into those, was sexier than seeing him naked.

So, that Monday was mine. The little possessiveness was bringing the wave of outlaws in me. I can hardly doubt if I ever tried to put boundaries for anyone before, even for a day. He was my first, my one man in billions, the shooting star only I got a chance to get a glance of. How could I not be possessive?

 It was him, I and our badass free spirits. I made him switch off his phone in my presence, and he was only allowed to turn it on if I got dead. Nobody cares enough to call me till date except my parents, and with age, the frequency of calls got downwards. Also I was never an important existence in anyone's life, and to be very true, I enjoy avoidance. Attention is such a vengeance for me.

I went to his house very early in the morning, told my mom that it was my friend's birthday, so I had to go to his house first, then college, then again to his house until the party was over. Mom was pretty impressed with my under-constructive social skills and supported me faithfully to blend into the society. I was social. Adith and I were friends first. Now, we are more than that. So, by that logic, I was more social and that was an upgrade.

I was so early for his house that I didn't see Mr. Sen strolling around the garden with his big, rusty watering can, and with the clacking of my new gladiator, it seemed like the whole alley finally woke up. I reached his room through the stairs carrying the shoes in my hand, trying to be as silent as possible. His eyes were grounded on the newspaper, got to feel my presence when I grappled his shoulders from behind. His smile wrinkled his eyes when I sat on his lap spreading my arms across his shoulder, ran my fingers through his hair and wrapped his lips with mine.

"Happy Day, Birthday Boy. I am your Santa Claus today. Make a wish."

He dabbed a kiss and said, "You."

I didn't prepare any impending reply for that, so I stumbled a bit and said, "I have something more than that."

He let me get released from his hug, and I started unfolding the things I got for him. He was my dark wind bae, my mystery man; I never got to know him to the core, but the far I knew I chose the gifts on some assumptions.

He was a huge fan of eau de colognes. His perfume and cologne collections could easily attract paid visitors. I don't know how he used to do that, but his smell was much different from those colognes- much better and real. He was my favorite smell. Like every time he was around me, I felt like breathing him more, and wished I could elude the outs. He possessed a charm, his existence was radioactive. The whiff of his bare skin is raw, heavenly and authentic. Every time I laid on his chest, I swear I wished the time would stop eternally; I wanted to inhale him for the end of the time- the far I could make it. Every little thing about him made me crazy, that dangerously crazy where you can smile on your own wreckage. He was like the song I found on a random shuffle that got stuck in my head like forever, and I lost the key of escaping it.

I bought him a cologne which sucked all my savings at once, a beige-colored pillow with his initials as it was his favorite color, a small jar of mango pickle which my grandma sent and a nicely folded letter surrendering myself to him like I was no longer an individual entity.

First, he read the letter, sat silent for a bit, looked up at me gradually and asked, "Kenny, if I tell you something today, would you believe me?"

I nodded.

"I can never be thankful enough to god to give me the best thing he has. I don't know how you did that, but will you laugh at me if I say I love you?"- I went nearer to him, hold his hands inside my crossed-fist, kissed him on his left cheek and let him finish. "I love you, Kenny. I am madly in love with you. Please find me palliatives before I collapse. It isn't right."

I didn't get everything he meant, but his eyes were damp. I felt his heart was burning in an unknown fear, and I didn't even guess any reason. We were together in love. It was a happy story. I saw no fear, no evil inside. But at that time, all I could hear was him, his soul speaking the soar, wanting me to be his solace for those moments.

I placed my chin on his left clavicle, near enough to reach his ears to whisper," Collapse into me, and I will never let you walk away."

"I know."- He hugged me even tighter.

We kept laying on his bed like this for hours. Then he chinned up and made my hair with his fingers and took me to the breakfast table. It was a wholesome Bengali breakfast with all my favorite stuff- Luchi, daal, Paneer, and a cranberry pie as dessert. That wasn't a real pie. It was a nice recipe of his guilt-free desserts made with all the cashews, walnuts, almonds, dates, whey protein, and cranberry; mainly it was a yummy blend made with the items you may find at home.

I was impressed to see the efforts he put to make me happy. It was supposed to be me who would be doing all the things for him, but he was more than the good one can expect in a human. I never learnt to love December before he came in. He made those flowers bloom again which were never supposed to live. His presence made me more human that I could ever plan to be.

Oh Adith! What you have done! Why have you done what you have done! What would be a me without you!

That was the day I lived worth thousand days of laying dead. He read me a story, sang me a song and he wasn't terrible. The food was delicious, the sex was amazing, and everything was at its threshold of perfection. He made the world breathable for me. He came from nowhere and lit up my darkness like I was never made to function without him, and for that instance, I didn't want to. He was the lover worth waiting for a lifetime. I was hooked, trapped, addicted to him and there was no place to step back.

The love-month never had a hit on me like that year. I had a lover and that was not a very usual thing for me. Being in love wasn't actually a burden like the world makes it look like. To me, it was a magic, a betterment of me, a responsibility of finding ways to make him happier more than the ways he could do. Like when a child starts growing up, no one needs to teach to love his parents. It comes from inside, in reflex, with time, with maturity. Just like the way I never stopped loving my parents, my brother, even at my worst days; my love for him was not any lesser than that. He was my every day. So, it didn't actually matter if it was February, or July. My graph of love started with a high value and if I assume the Y-axis as time, my X value for him increased every day making the inclination more positive than it used to be yesterday.

13th February morning was softly warm. The necessity of sweaters was dying slowly. Streets were getting younger with lights, colors, glitters, newly-drawn graffiti and most importantly with the crowd. The couples who just had started dating, the couples who had overcome long tough years together, the couples who were engaged, the couple who got broken once and again fixed things for better, even the couple who were on the last chapter of their lives and still holding hands like the first day they expressed love- all were on the streets to celebrate their valentine with others. It was a scene to admire, to cherish and to feel happy for those who made it.

In all those years of puberty, my hatred for Valentine's Day was insanely strong. Can't say I was totally wrong, but to be very honest, I was more jealous than angry. I saw everyone happy but me; had a lover but me, and how special they are to them. I used to shut the door and lock my windows so that I couldn't get a glance of people holding hands or kissing each other. I hated the idea of not being special in anyone's life, not even for a moment. Ishaan never made me feel like I was anything more than just a whizz in his life and all I have learnt from that relationship is what not to do in a relationship. My childhood was abducted by the fear of not being perfect and catching an eye while existing, and I failed at both. Being Kanishk's sister wasn't any easy and not being a brilliant mind like him never let me be free from the judgments of the society and sometimes from my own relatives. Everybody saw me smiling in front of them, but nobody heard me crying. Crying to make the monsoon ashamed of its own capabilities; crying through the way the thunder rumbling in my heart. The pain of being left out and unwanted tore me so bad that some days I used to put a black cover on my mirror, trying to avoid the fact of being alive. I didn't want to be seen, even by me.

I hated my face, my body, my existence- my everything. If I didn't book the cab that day, maybe I would've killed myself by now.

Being with Adith never felt like modern math. We were easy. We loved ourselves the way like it wasn't ever complicated. We used to have fights but we both were mature enough to bring it to the table and find a way to end it with a pun. It was almost a year of having him and I was still grateful to him every single day for loving and wanting me in a way I was never loved and wanted before.

That 13th was special for me. That was the first time I was allowed to buy a Valentine's present. After all those years of passing my 14th laying on bed and embarking on the successful female figures who are either divorced or never thought of having a man in their life, I never got the feeling of letting one in. I thought about a lot of gifts but nothing seemed perfect enough to finalize. So, I went to the common way to buy a shirt. I knew his preferences so it wasn't that hard.

I drove across the way to the south city mall which was a 15 min drive from his house and far more from mine, and had a plan to pay a visit to his house afterwards. That week we didn't meet even once. Somebody died in my college, so it was closed for 3 days and my mom had to write the condolences to post, so there were no ways to lie. The other days my house was occupied as my aunts came along and mom wanted an extra hand for help. So, it was an unusual long gap which made my longing for him even stronger.

In the mall, I saw a lot of couples hanging out, buying stuff for each other, going to movie halls, enjoying a couple massage, and doing all the things I never did. Adith and I didn't go out at all. All the stuff we had done, we had done at home. Every time I made a plan for us to go anywhere, he came up with a better plan of staying back and enjoying at home.

Some days I was untamable, subtly wild like a metal-head with a guitar, not powered to be dimmed with any. Those days he took my head on his lap and adored my hair with his gentle fingertips until I fall asleep. Some days I was his best girl, inhaling and sticking to the scent of summer in his skin until the clock left me behind. Maybe I wasn't missing anything. Maybe it was the best thing that most of the couples regret missing. And in that case, I was the gainer. Adith fulfilled me in every way and I shouldn't be whining over my selfish senses.

Some mornings carry the gracefulness itself when one can't assume the sight of the devil. The 13th morning wasn't any different than that. It was sunny, preppy and was carrying a festive smell all around. I bought a shirt for him, danced a bit, had a pizza and was oscillating my feet under the food court table while crushing down a big bite. I was supposed to finish my coke and go out to see Adith after a while and thrust the shirt in his hand a day earlier cause my excitements weren't staying in limits. It was 1:12, my phone screen lit up with a Whatsapp notification. It was from him, but unlike every time it didn't bring a smile on my face, rather it made my blood clot to death, and throat shore with the fear of reality. In that warmth of nature, my body temperature dropped so low that anybody could have mistaken me as dead by touching me at once. I opened our chat box to confirm if I was reading it right.

"I am leaving.
It's over.
Please, do not connect back."
First few seconds, I was trying to figure out its meaning sarcastically. But soon, I found no sarcasm at all when I texted back a *"What"* and that didn't get delivered. There's no DP,

there's no bio, there's no double-tick and in conclusion, there's no him. I tried to call but the IVR tone said I somehow had dialed a wrong number which was saved in my phonebook for almost a year. For some moments, I was still trying to figure out if I said something offensive in the last few days and hurt him somehow. But from my side, there was none. Neither I could find any, from his words. Our relationship never faltered upon some silly words, and that's where I lost the missing piece of the puzzle, forever.

After some time of defeating my negativities in a false route, all I got was the idea of reaching his place and clearing out everything between us. I left my unfinished coke right where I started slurping, and rushed to the parking lot to get up and make it to him. His valentine shirt was still in the paper bag hanging from my elbow and my hopes weren't in the mood of giving up and taking things back to the rat-hole I started.

The 15 minutes' drive took me only six and half minutes to cover, and reaching there, all I could glance over was the tired face of Mr.Sen. He saw me coming from a distance and still did not care enough to open the gate for me. I ran all the way from the parking place to his couch. He was resting, extending his neck on the edge of the soft couch and when my footsteps became more prominent, he only muttered, "He's gone."

"Why? When? Did you try to stop him?"

"He was gone before I could open my eyes. I didn't see him going; neither could I hear any squeak. He left the next month's rent on my table and probably didn't want me to see him go."- He didn't move from his resting place.

"But why? Did he say something to you yesterday or any day? I can't see any reason to leave like this?"

"No."

"Did you try calling him?"

"Like you don't? His number is non-existent. Go home, young lady. If I am right, he's not gonna come back. Don't ask me why cause I don't know. Drive safe or if possible ask anyone else to drive you home. I don't think you are in a condition to make it to your home safely. And yes, close the gate after you leave. Nowadays the stray dogs are entering anywhere."

My nose was already runny as I was trying to hide my tears by sucking it back. For those moments, I was dead. Everything in front of me was turning into black, an eternal black- powerful enough to engulf me. My breaths were pumping faster, struggling to stay in pace. I was trying to imagine a world without him which was going to be the new normal from that very moment. Finally a tear rolled down to my cheek ignoring all my efforts to hold it back. I turned around, and said a "Thank You" to Mr. Sen in a steady voice suppressing my sobs. I closed the gate and held it heartily for the last time. From now on, there would be no morning disturbance, no window escapes, no modern pops, and no upstairs' noises. Mr. Sen must be happy and in peace while I was gonna miss his annoyed stares while leaving without closing the hinges of his gate. Maybe the place was crying too, for being quiet again and erasing all the year-long emotions in just a few moments. This is how gravity of existence matters. Just one single person gagged the life of a place along with two other people together without saying or hearing a word. This is how the cruelty of life is defined and I had no option but to accept it. With or without him, life goes on.

MY NOTE

The winter weeks are often faster, but that year, it didn't leave until I was too broke to heal. A whole month had passed and hence it felt the same. I was stuck right there where he left me- unveiled and barely alive.

I had tried a thousand times to connect him somehow, but along with his phone number, he was non-existent as well. Mr. Sen had my number and was told to inform me if he saw Adith standing at his door, drenched in apologies. I knew he was never gonna come back, but my heart never stopped hoping. He was gone to the impossible where my love wasn't strong enough to bring him back. He used to talk about the ways I had to live if there were no him. Not for a single second of that universe, I imagined those were practicalities. I was so in love with the idea of being with him, I never thought he wasn't joking. And that's where the clash began- the clash between desires and reality. My mind was at a war and of course, I was losing it every day.

That evening the sky broke down into splashes to touch the ultimate horizon. It wasn't supposed to rain after a sunny day when I was daydreaming of having my previous life back with him. Enjoying the lively mornings together, sneaking into his house, intentionally misplacing his bookmarks and seeing him not getting mad, enjoying the cuddles, feeling the fire in my skin when his touch used to melt down my hormones, crossing the deadlines to come home, escaping from his window and coming again next morning without bothering Mr. Sen's gloomy glimpses, and a hell lot of things that turned into a lie in a moment. I was still trying to find an answer to all the *'why'*s his disappearance planted in my head! There were no plausible excuses for him leaving the way he did. I was still prattling if I did something wrong, but unable to find any.

I was watching the rain shower holding my face with both the hands supported by the elbow on my desk. My eyes were dry, running out of tears. Days were much easier to survive, but nights left me incomplete without howling. I never shrieked, neither did I look for a therapist to listen to my story and give me sympathy. I became my own listener. Sometimes I cried silently, sometimes I waited for my parents to leave the house so that I could cry as loud as possible. Sometimes I was in college, in the middle of a lecture and ran to the washroom to cry my brains out keeping the tap running, therefore came back with red eyes faking the sneezes and false cough in my throat. I never wanted anyone to know I was dying. I prefer seeing jealousy rather than reflecting sympathy for me in someone's eyes. I don't wanna be seen, bothered, cared or tolerated. I am better off burning alone.

The night came to my place a little earlier than the day. Noon flashed, gone in a moment. I was still sitting by the window, unbothered, unloved and unrequited. I tried to cry, but there were no tears left. So, I tried to be bled by the words- took my pen from the case, and started clustering my confessions in a letter.

"Dear whoever get this letter, cause I don't know whom to address first,

It's been long since I talked to anyone properly, so writing this feels like inhaling some fresh air. I don't know who you are and how badly you are going to judge me, but when you will get this, I will probably be dead. I have given it a thought and couldn't find any other way to survive. Suicide is my only survival. I've chosen it on my own. None has influenced or forced me to do so.

I was in love with a boy from last year and it's turning a year in a few months. My love was deep, dark, desirable, and dangerous. I never wanted to lose him but somehow, he slipped away. I realized my feelings weren't strong enough to make him stay. There was something inside his head, stronger than my love and that drove him away from me. It's not that I am leaving my life because he left me behind, but I am leaving for a lot of valid reasons. I don't know where to start, but I feel like I should make myself clear before being silent forever.

I am the younger child of my parents and I don't know how dumb of them to have me after having an amazing kid like my brother, Kanishk. I remember every time he knocked me down just because the dividing line between us is noticeable. I was never like him and never could I become. God has blessed him with a brilliant brain and a mean heart, and cruelly gave me the opposite.

He was a school topper, college topper and hopefully he will gonna clear this UPSC attempt too. The more I was proud of being his sibling, the more he was ashamed of being mine. I clearly remember the time Kanishk's friends came over and got shocked to know that he has a sister, after all those years of knowing him as a single child of my parents. The more shocking thing was nobody scolded him, said nothing. Everything went back to normal after they left and nobody brought that into the table till today. I was 13, and from that day, I started realizing my value in this house- to be descriptive, I was not any greater than those old music CDs in the showcase- unless it's a good day, nobody thinks of me and sometimes they try to hide my existence when modern-generation heavy metal takes over. I never complained about that. Brothers are supposed to be brutal and adjusting with him was a part of my sisterhood. My nana taught me that and she wasn't totally wrong.

After all these years of compromising my part of life, I am tired of being the only one who is trying and not getting anything in return. I am tired of people treating me like trash. Almost everyone who came to my life has played a big role of making me absorb the uselessness of my existence, and how unfortunate they would be if somehow my company warms them.

I remember every time I was too modest to say 'No' to the plans I wasn't even a bit interested in. I remember all the funds I broke to help my friends who wanted urgent cash and how stupidly I never asked them back and how gently they never cared to return them. I remember how badly I made myself available to those who deserved not even a seat beside me. And later I found out those spreading lies on my name just because somehow I hurt their self-esteem by sharing the things they did to me to the people I thought had befriended me. I was wrong and unlucky at the same time. My luck never worked while looking for a quality friendship and love I was famished for. Even though I tried giving my world to them, that was never enough. On the edge of the priorities, I was like a one-night stand- they threw me out when the night was over.

If I come to my family, I am probably the unluckiest sibling on earth whose brother is deeply ashamed of recalling the day I was born. Even after having a brother, I never got love, affection from him. And as an amazing fact, none of my family members are bothered about why we do not have a healthy relationship like others. As Kanishk used to bring home medals, certificates and appreciations, all his cruelty drained out like it never existed. Not only have my parents, all my friends' parents taken Kanishk as a paradigm of success. They want their child to be like him, which is my worst nightmare. I don't wanna be like him. I wanna be me. An individual. A different identity. I am sick of people calling me

Kanishk's sister and look into me with pity in their eyes. Does being a topper bring heaven in life? None of the Billionaires today can say that the money comes from any of their degrees, and I think I would never know. This is not what I was supposed to say, but I am feeling a little dizzy. Don't know how long I could go on, but before I reach the ceiling, I want to confess everything.

It's true that the relationship between Kanishk and I is toxic. The moment God dropped me into his life, he hated me to the bones. He never wanted to be a brother and even if he wanted, I think he would never choose me as his sister. He hates me and I can strongly feel that. But to the core of my heart, there are still some loves left for him, and as Nana told, I think I would never stop loving him even if he ever comes to murder me. I don't know why he never accepted me as his sister and what problems I have created by existing in his life. Mom and dad love him the most and I have no problem with that. But Kanishk, if you are reading this as a sign of respect to my dead soul, can you tell me why you never picked me up when I fell on the ground and was crying for help? It was the third-grade annual sports day. You were on eighth, old enough to come forward and took me to the sister for medicines. I remember I was crying and calling your name as I saw you hiding behind those trees but you went away with your friends. You never came, but Nikhil did. And look at me, standing today, I don't have any of you. It's a tragedy, right?

We weren't the only brother and sister studying in the same school, there were many. And I saw all of them taking care of each other with love, holding each other's back and sharing tiffins when their benches got empty in a half-day. You never even cared to visit me or return home with me for a single day. You left me in the school without an umbrella when they declared it a rainy day after the first period. You came back home and told nobody I was still there waiting for someone to come and take me home. I was there alone, crying in the heavy rain and thunder for

3 hours until Mom came back and noticed I was missing. Why Kanishk? Why do you hate me so much? Because I can't get the topper medal like you every year? Or I can't solve Rubik's cube as fast as you do? Why? I always loved you after all these things you did to me, so why not you? Why can't you love me, Kanishk? Even for a day? Am I that unlovable?

For Nikhil, I don't know whether to be mad at you or to say goodbye for the last time with love. The responsibilities I expected from my brother, you fulfilled them all without asking anything in return. All the blocks Kanishk left hollow, you filled them with love. Nikhil, you are my best friend, best brother and the best shoulder to lean on. I found peace when you came to my life and taught me to live without being perfect. Till I had you, everything was good, sound and rich. But when you left, I feel like every good thing is leaving me gradually. I love you, Nik. You know how much you mean to me, and still, you choose to leave. After you get that girl in your college, you barely talk to me. It felt like I was forcing you to keep the connection every time, and when I stopped calling, you never called me back. Till today, there's none from your side. I am angry, jealous, sad and rancid. You've pushed me away, you've killed our friendship, and now in the moment of dying I am still cherishing those. I don't know why you did this, but for me, you are still my best friend and I can't explain how badly I miss you every day. My regret of not having you in my last days will always haunt me, maybe even after today, when I will be dead. Goodbye Nik, have a great life.

For Mom, I love you. You know, how much I love you. You mean the world to me. Sometimes I lied to you for escaping a couple of hours behind your eyes. You may get angry, but I never meant to hurt you by those lies. Those are healthy. I hope you didn't mind that I did. Just please don't cry seeing me hanging from the ceiling. Even when I am dead, I can hear you cry and every tear from your eyes will hit me like taking millions of bullets altogether. You are my life, Mom. So, never feel void when I am gone. My love will remain the same as before, around you, filling you always.

For Dad, you know you are the man of my life. Nothing in the world can ever explain my love for you. Pisi says we have so much similarities that anyone can understand we are dad and daughter even after seeing us for the first time. You have never been rude to me and I can't express how lucky I am for being your daughter. But this is the high time. I have to leave. Everything that is surrounding my guts making me suffocated. Sometimes, I can't breathe properly. I feel like losing this battle with me. I am strong as a competitor and simultaneously I am terribly easy to be defeated. I am defeated this time, Daddy. I am thirsty, starved, broken and empty. My body is quitting but my love doesn't. I love you and I will love you till my soul manages to survive even by parts, a little. I am leaving, Dad. Don't cry and waste your tears on such a waste like me, and if possible, please forgive me for fleeing. You have done more than any other dad can ever do. I love you and I will love you always.

Last but not the least, the guy I loved every moment in my last one year. I don't want to reveal his name but I am leaving this note for him, just in case he ever comes to my door and seeks my whereabouts. Tell him I loved him from the very first day we met, and I had never stopped loving him even at these last moments. He was the moon of my starless life and when he was gone, my life had become some deviant raft of a losing battle. If you think I am leaving because he left me, it's wrong. It's absolutely wrong. Yes, I am hurt, but I ain't suicidal for him.

I am just tired. Tired of everything. I can't keep up the drama of being alive every day. I am not well, Mom. I know you felt it. I am dying inside. Years full of hatred, pity, failures, rejections are killing me. I can no longer live like this. My journey with you guys ends today. I am privileged I got you as my family. Tell Kanishk, I don't hate him, but if he ever touches my diaries, I would start doing that too.

Today I am releasing you guys from the burden of being my parent. I am freeing my brother from the blood relation he always wanted to omit from his life. I am letting my best friend go to the world of better people where there is fun, parties, colours and lives. He no longer needs to listen to my sad stories just because he's polite. You are free from the thoughts of making me a better person. I failed myself not because I am lacking anything, but I am more than the world can make a room for. The days are getting heavier and I am afraid I can no longer weigh it with me.

Burn me with my notebooks. I want to be the ash assorted with my own creations. Goodbye everyone! I wish I will meet you again one day- inside different frames, as different persons, in a different universe. Let me go with peace.

Kenny"

My pen stopped there. I could write a novel about how it was storming inside me, but I chose not to. I was scared that if I made it too long, nobody would read it at all. I just confessed some sugar-coated truth just the way they needed to hear them. But my heart was still stumbling upon the fact of leaving my mom and dad in a world without me. My dad always wanted a daughter, and when I was born, I heard he threw a party of being a girl-dad. He didn't do it for Kanishk, he did it for me. For him, I was special and leaving him like that was ripping my heart apart. But there was no other choice. I touched all my things for the very last time; my clothes, my makeup, my shoes, my childhood photos, and most importantly my notes.

I came to the table and started waiting for the evening to fall down. My dizziness caught my senses and I couldn't realize when I fell asleep on my desk resting my head on my crossed hands, not for the last time.

A gentle hand on my shoulder, grabbed my skin tight, like a haul in my mizzen mast. It awakened me in seconds and took me to the world of survival again. I first checked the letter. It was under my palm and not visible to any who would walk through the door. I slowly looked back and blinked a few times to confirm what I was seeing was there for real! First few seconds, I was shocked, but then I finally started believing it.

It was Nikhil; but from a different world. A faceful of unmade beard, comparatively longer hair, tanned skin, and apologetic eyes.

"Kenny"- That rudeness was gone. His voice was humble, shaky, soft and numb.

I didn't say anything in return.

"Can you stand up for me?"- I was still sitting on the chair tapping my toes on the floor under my desk and my face wasn't ceasing to be wondrous. It was really hard to pretend why he cut off all the connections and never cared to look back for 7-8 months and suddenly all emotions flashed on, and he showed up in my room silently, asking me to stand up! Weird! Everything was weird.

I stood up though and then all of a sudden I felt his weight on me, nudged my whole body from a former equilibrium. He hugged me so tightly that I had to take out my left hand to grab the desk as a support.

"Kenny, I am sorry. I am so sorry. I miss you. It was all my fault! I am sorry, Kenny. Please be my bro again."

I wasn't ready for these much shocks altogether. Nikhil was in my room, hugging me and mumbling apologies. His hug was so tight, I wasn't able to get rid of it unless he wanted me to, and whenever I was trying to lose out, he was grabbing me even harder. Even in those breath-taking moments, I felt a little relief - the relief of having him back. The hug was something I was missing for a long time, and again he came to fill me up at the right moment.

"Nik, I understand. Leave me, please. You are gonna strangle me otherwise. Leave, I can't breathe properly."- I finally said.

He loosened me up. I finally take a deep, long breath. He sat on my bed and I sat on my chair. I didn't know how to or where to start and whether to ask why he was gone for that long and if he was planning to do that again! After these long months of detachment, I couldn't be sure if he was my same old pal with a judgement-free zone or he was someone else whom I didn't know at all.

For a minute, there was a gagging silence. Then he spoke up.

"You are angry. Aren't you?"

I nodded.

"You were right. I am an asshole. I am that stupid douchebag that dumped his best friend for a bitch. I don't deserve your forgiveness, ain't I?"

"She's a bitch now? A few days ago, she was everything you needed. Now what? She dumped you?"

"She's married, Kenny. And she didn't tell me. I was in jail for 3 days. You wanna know why? Her husband pressed a kidnapping charge on me, when we were out for a weekend trip. Demanded 10 lakhs for not pressing a false rape case. Dad bailed me out and paid them to withdraw all the charges against me. I am ruined, Kenny. Principal's decision is pending on whether to keep me in college or to rusticate me. When I was at the edge of ending my life, thinking about everyone who never doubted me, the only visible face on my mind was yours. I was mistaken. I fell in her web. Please take me back, Kenny. I want my previous life back."

I saw him crying. The tears of shame were rolling down his throat, wet his beard and kept flowing. I didn't know what to say, but at least the Nikhil I knew was much different than the one who was crying in front of me. He was no longer the proud sod. He was gentle, humble and not afraid to express his emotions.

Therefore, the question came in my female instinct, wasn't appropriate. It was probably the rudest thing to ask him, but I couldn't help. I didn't actually judge the parameter of rudeness or disbelief in it. I just asked.

"Did you rape her?"

He looked at me calmly. His red eyes didn't show any anger or any other emotion. He was as serene as before with little teardrops in his deep ocean eyes.

"Do you think I did that?" - His voice shook up.

"Nik, I never thought you would leave me for some other woman. You did that, so what you are expecting me to believe now! You were away from me for a long time. How can I know what you did and what you didn't?"

"Kenny, if I touch you with your consent, is that a rape?"

"No."- I said lowering my eyes.

"She made me believe that she loved me. More than anything in her life. I loved her, Kenny. I didn't know she was married. She never ever told me that. We were like a couple. How can I rape her? Please explain. And I don't think my mom raised a rapist. I would rather kill myself before harassing a woman. I didn't do anything and I can still commit to you that I would never do that to a woman, ever. I am not a creep, Kenny. I can never be that worst."

It was true. I can't clearly pretend the number of times Nikhil saved my ass from being assaulted in public transport. The middle-aged assaulters are everywhere. Whenever we were together, he guarded me like a hawk. I remember once he punched a guy in the face who was trying to grope me in a metro station. In no possible excuses, I can believe Nikhil can touch a woman without her consent.

India is more into feminists now, to be mentioned, into pseudo feminists, who have nothing to contribute to the society rather than asking for rights to roam naked. And if I ask about the responsibilities they should take and the contributions they should make for a better India, they rather choose to ignore the subject. Both the real and false rape cases are upwards. Rapists are always to be punished brutally, but for me, the punishments should be the same for those women who put false charges on men to make them suicidal or to take tons of money as a bribe for hiding the crime they didn't commit. If you want equality, see it from both sides. This is also a responsibility of a real feminist to reveal the reality of those women who align false cases on men just to thrive. Just as we raise our voices against a rapist and his death sentence, we should do the same for those women who make others' lives miserable when proven. Criminals don't have a gender. They are guilty and that should be their only identity. And for them, punishments shouldn't be gender-biased.

"I believe you. But now what? You are free from charges. Everyone's going to forget this in a month or two. Everything will be alright. Don't overthink. You want a coffee?"

"Do you really think that? Oh God! I never thought the place of my dreams would become a nightmare one day."- He put both his hands on his face and wiped those tears roughly.

"How about you? How have you been? How's Adithya? He's alright?"

I looked at him and took a pause. While listening to his story, somehow I lost into it. I forgot I had a broken life which was tragic enough to nudge me into suicide. An hour ago, I wrote everyone a letter of confession before death. Now, Nikhil's story made me realize how badly wrong I was. If my life was in a nutshell, what can I call Nikhil's? He was drowning in shame, guilt, and resentment. His career was on the wreck. The girl he loved did something that any guy can hardly imagine in their scariest dreams. Suddenly my problems seemed so less in front of his. And I was trying to quit my life on those fudgy excuses! What was wrong with me? Why was I being so selfish? The people I was tried leaving were the people I loved the most.

That was the moment of turning back. No, I wasn't leaving, I would never do that. *I will fight and I will live till the last day to see the games I have changed on my own. I won't be a fugitive. I would rather fight to lose.*

That night Nikhil stayed in my house. We talked about almost everything. He fell asleep in my arms and I didn't complain how heavy his head felt on my skinny biceps. He listened to me, consoled me and we chucked silence together. Every shade of emotions felt so real that night. I was no longer feeling the unwanted, useless waste in the world. Nikhil remembered me when the whole world refused to trust him back. I was his trustee, his brother, his best friend, his only friend who brought down the rain again to heal his drought cracks. I was so happy he was there, into my arms, sleeping like a new-born. We were friends again. We got our old days back. What a hell of a night!

My mom approached his mom to let him stay with us until he was ready to move back. My mom never doubted him for a second and offered him to live with us even after knowing he was just got accused for a kidnapping case a few weeks ago. I never felt so privileged and honoured before, for being a daughter of this woman. She is the lady of my life. And by her decisions, I owed her everything.

ADVENTURE NEXT DOOR

"**K**enny, open the door."- I don't know why Nikhil never shows any respect to the existence of our doorbell, and shakes the whole equilibrium of our house with one shriek every time he comes. From childhood to instance, the graph of the magnitude of his shriek is on positive inclination. Even my neighbors find his voice so irritating that none of our loud gossips have enough audiences from their sneaky balconies.

I go downstairs and open the door.

"Hey, I got you some sizzler brownie with loads of vanilla ice cream."- His wide smile and innocent intention restrained me from yelling at him.

Six months have passed since Adith's departure from my life; a lot of things have changed and made me stronger enough not to get afraid of changes again. At the very beginning, my emotional dumb-ass heart refused to stay normal. Losing him was never easy and every single night paid the price of it. I was crazy about him. I still do, but time creates every remedy to cure your wounds.

Without him, life seemed so less that eating, sleeping and interacting with friends and family became a burden to me. The visible changes in my physique and my behavior caught Nikhil's attention first and he took me to a therapist. Though I never thought I was insane enough to call in a therapist, but who could ever win over Nikhil and his rigid decisions?

But soon Nikhil took his trust off from the healthcare system after scrolling his eyes on the number of antidepressants the *so-called* therapist prescribed. I was neither crazy nor depressed; I was extremely void inside out. My feelings died, and talking it out loud was never a wise option. All I needed was some fresh air and a break from being a normal child every day. The way I was brought up in a restrictive household, I was never taught to show my cry for help even if I am damaged or high. So, how can I clear up my wound now if I don't know how to look for some cure? The very time I used to tell my story to Nik, my tears never got dried.

The way he left, throwing my feelings away with some inert words, I should be angry or hateful. But every day I lay on my bed looking at the window, I couldn't help but hope that he will return to my window pane with some underhand, silent knocks, tell me it was all a lie and he still loves me more than the way he shows. I wonder how madly I am still obsessed with him from the very first day we exchanged smiles. His touch was so intense that it's still very palpable when I remember those neck kisses, those sun rays, those last bites of ice cream and his eyes when he smiles.

These days are making me go to college, having drawing lessons, and helping mom in her household work with a restful mind. I am not that mad to yell on baseless stuff endlessly like before, so I have stopped talking to Kanishk. Hanging out with Nikhil never felt so needed before, but wandering around alone feels like breathing some fresh air, because that's the time you realize letting go of a desired lifetime with someone you love, is the worst feeling you can afford to fight. Reality is so harsh and so does the male emotion. I could never find any possible sequence about how God made these males so firm with all the power of endurance and never cared to put some into female dignity.

"Why the hell on earth did you buy sizzler in a plastic container? And why don't you ever buzz the bell? If you shout from the next time, I swear I won't open the door."

"Shut up. The ice cream has started melting. Give me a bowl right now."

I take two bowls from the fridge and serve the ice cream with chocolate sauce and Winnie-the-pooh-printed-spoon, which Nikhil gifted on my birthday. I put some cranberries on his ice cream to make his bowl a little fancier than mine, cause Nikhil is one of those mannered brats who like fine-dining over a messy buffet.

"Nik, I am thinking of going somewhere. Would you like to join?"

Nikhil was about to overrun another spoonful of ice cream, but he stopped there, moved his head dramatically forward, squeezed his eyes like a dominant parent to make me recall all the stupid proposals I have ever made to him. Then he evenly said, "Where?"

"To Mr.Sen's house. Adith's Landlord- Ravi Mohan Sen."

The hatred for Adith Nikhil weighs in his heart always scares me to express my feelings in front of him. He is always so hypercritical and discriminating against my stupid emotions, and probably thinks I am just a lost cause in the world of ample opportunities. But a loner like me isn't blessed with too many friends to talk to, to share things with, so whatever happens to my vigorous senses, I always have to make a head down to Nikhil, doesn't matter how many times he gets annoyed to be my listener and rescue me out if I am drowning.

I was expecting a rejection and some solid reason about why I should hate Adith and shouldn't be thinking about him any longer; but no: Nikhil actually said, "You aren't over him yet, do you? Seems like the tricky dude did some actual magic on you. Okay, let's go where you are thinking to, but what would we do there? The far I know he's long gone. Sometimes, I wonder if he was a true wizard from Hogwarts and after getting bored of you, he went back to his world through platform 9^3/4. Should we search in the railway stations? What you think?"

"Nik, I am serious. Stop pulling me right now. I just wanna see his place again, if by chance he left something important there or the memories hit me back. It will be a nice visit I promise. So tomorrow?"

"Hence…..yeah"

I didn't expect convincing Nik would be this easy, especially when it's about the guy he never wants me to be with. So, when I got the affirmation, I started getting ready from the previous night to invade into Adith's place with a proper chronology. I thought of taking my folded ladder from my playhouse which used to work as a tool to fix the roof of my playhouse itself, but suddenly it made me realize how badly I have grown up these years, physically and mentally that it no longer can take me to the roof even at my thinnest. Nikhil discoursed to use the stairs silently after reassuring the age and marital status of Mr.Sen, cause you can't always expect an unmarried old man to be very sound-sensitive for his visitors.

We reached there at 7 in the morning as Adith used to say that Mr.Sen wakes up late after struggling hard to sleep every lonely night. Somehow, I still have the spare key of his room as I used to go there very often, mostly in the evening for our friendly and sexual encounter. Mr.Sen used to go for an evening walk daily and I was fit enough to jump through the ropes and sunshades by the time we were done. But when we were in a mood, we better prefer to spend the day in a hotel away from the fear of getting caught for doing nothing illegal except trespassing in my boyfriend's house.

The main gate wasn't a great hurdle to cross as Mr.Sen keeps it clear and rust-free with regular cleaning and oiling, and it doesn't make awakening sounds while opening. Reaching inside, I got a bit of relief to see that he didn't get enough time to change the locks and the key of that lock, which was jingling in my pocket, was still a fit-in. Nik stood there to admire how amazingly vibrant and organized his garden was and under the green shed of foliage, even summer isn't summery enough without any air conditioner. Mr.Sen was probably in his mid-sleep then, so we quickly unlocked the main door and went upstairs barefoot as my gladiator and Nik's boot could be loud enough to wake Mr.Sen up.

The second floor was Adith's kingdom. Mr.Sen was very choosy for his paying guests and he didn't allow a lot of people to come and visit. So, not everyone gets to stay in his house even after accepting his high rents at the first proposal. He must've seen something in Adith that made him confirming his stay in just one discussion. These two had some closer connection, and I never tried to know how Mr.Sen is now spending his days without yelling at Adith to bathe and eat on time.

Again, I noticed that he didn't care to change the lock of Adith's room and the duplicate key again successfully opened the door without making any hassle. His room was the most regular place I loved to come to and the forged part of keeping it secret and silent, made it more exciting. So, opening the door rejuvenated all my rusty memories and the layers of soft dusts on his desk and in the corners of his bed, kind of doomed my spirits. The bed was perfectly organized with a new bed sheet and some soft cushions, one of which I bought for Adith; but there was no one to make it into a real use. This bed is the witness of a lot of storms, hopes, tears, and uncertainties. It had seen love and lies. Even after all these times, its puffiness felt the same and somehow it still smelt like Adith. Maybe he kept some of his essence in this room for today; for me to come back and feel it. Maybe Nikhil is right. He's a wizard who knows my every vice and virtue and can see me every time from everywhere if he wants too.

"So, what should we do now? Stand back and admire how amazingly Mr.Sen did the cleaning."

"Nope, rather check if there's something in this room that can be interesting."

"Interesting? Like what?"

"I don't know. Just shut your mouth and switch on your torch."

Nik's face clearly reflected his disinterest in this witch-hunt. But I just wanted to give it a try to carry something from there as a memory. After a few moments, Nik called me pretty loudly and showed me a little keychain with some keys he found under the wardrobe. It was totally covered with dust and wasn't easy to catch an eye, but Nik's eyes are always on the needle point.

While we were figuring out where will be the locks of those different keys, an additional ray of torch fell on our faces and we clearly heard:

"What are you two little bastards doing in my house? You came here to steal something? Let me call the police first."

It was Mr.Sen and his crackling voice that broke our silence. When we finally realized that he was seriously gonna call the police, I readily switched on the light and uncovered the head-cap of my hoodie. He took some time to process where he had seen my face and why I was looking so familiar to him. Then he finally said:

"YOU! I know you. You are some Mukherjee, Adithya's sneaky girlfriend who used to make my sunshades muddy with her big-foot jumps. Do you know how much I needed to spend to clear my sunshades just for your ridiculous and failed attempt to keep your encounters confidential? You stupid girl! What do you think? I never noticed that you used to come often in the evening and leave at night through the window? I am so disappointed to see such a pretty and smart girl like you, are nothing but a big failure to fool a sick and lonely old man like me. This whole generation is stupid. Who's this frog-faced boy with you? Your brother? But you don't look similar?"

I didn't know how to respond. He called me pretty, smart and stupid at the same time. I was even more awestruck seeing him knowing me and my window-escapes pretty perfectly. I used to take the leap from the sunshades and might have scrunched some leaves underfoot, but he never let us know that he was watching my footsteps and allowing me to meet his *Adithya* even in the restricted hours. He just deflated all my confidence in a moment which I gathered after all those successful escapes. He calls Adith- *Adithya;* as *Adithya* is more Bengali than Adith and according to him, Adith is hell of a short name to call properly.

"Sir! I am so glad you remember me. This is my best friend Nikhil, we just came here to…."I was clearly stammering like I do in my viva exam and Nikhil was confused whether to laugh or to be offended for getting called a frog-face.

"What's your first name again?"

"Kiyana; Kiyana Mukherjee"

"Yeah, right. Adithya used to talk about you a lot and suddenly he was gone. Whatever, you people like some tea? Come on down, I am making. And this friend of yours, Nikhil! Is he deaf? Why is he looking at me like I stole his words?"

I jabbed Nikhil roughly. The wonder in his face wasn't about to ease. He was probably thinking how highly sarcastic Mr.Sen was and how his easy words made two urging youth cleanly bold even after asking for a tea. Nikhil still remained silent and sore, so I accepted his tea invitation and he chose us to sit in his garden where there were some beautiful sheds and some strikingly decorated table-chair underneath.

After few moments, Mr.Sen came with a big tray and joined our awkwardness. He brought some homemade orange croissants, roasted cashews and green tea. I am much familiar with the delicious taste of the croissants as he used to serve it as an evening snack for Adith, and I used to eat the most of it. Adith did like oranges but he didn't like it as a flavor if it's been put in any other thing, so I was in charge of not wasting anything just because Adith's picky attitude towards foods.

He served it very neatly with an additional glass of water. Then he started," What makes you visit this poor old man again? Your boyfriend is no longer here, so what you two were doing in his room?"

"I know. He left long ago and like you, I am also in the dark about the reasons. I came here to know the things you know about him and I don't."

"I don't think there's something like that. You people were always together and you think I may know something about him that you don't? What you think- I am his caretaker? He was my paying guest. Though I adored him like my own child, he lost that place when he left and cared to let me know just a few minutes ago. He kept the envelope of rent on my swing and left like I never mattered. Kids these days are really complicated and self-centered, but I didn't know he was one of them. Wait a minute, he didn't tell you either?"

"Nope, he just told me he is leaving, nothing more. That's why I am here to ask you more about him. It feels like we were together for months, most of the time in a day, and he is still a stranger to me."

"That dude is a complete mystery."- Nikhil said glumly.

"He definitely was. I can never say he talked a lot, but when he used to, I never felt any conundrum in him. Nevertheless, you never know someone by the way he shows himself in front of the world. Everything can be forged."-There were some disappointments in his voice.

"You are the landlord; you should have his details while assigning the rent. Can I see it, please?"- I said "Please" in such a fake way that even Nik looked at me with a disgusted face.

Mr.Sen didn't look so bothered and he leaned against the pillow of the chair even more comfortably and said," You think this is a mess or a boy's hostel? I just asked for his driving license and Aadhar even after he started staying here, and he gave me a Xerox copy of his license but I didn't ask for the Aadhar again. And I strongly doubt that the driving license can lead you to him because I never heard him talking about his house or parents, not even in any reference."

"Me neither. I just know Maharashtra is his own place, but where the hell am I gonna find him among 120 million people there."- My excitement rushed so quickly that I failed to maintain a proper manner by adding "hell" between the conversation with an old man. Though Mr.Sen didn't pay attention to my words, a thousand judgments were passed from Nikhil. I knew some big speeches were waiting for me when I was gonna get out of that yard.

"Means you are still looking for him! Well kid, I will advise you something and it's your choice to take it or not. I have spent all my youth chasing a woman and I ended up hurting myself again and again. The people who are meant to be with you, they will find a way to reach you for a lifetime, not just for a day. Forever is an illusion and I don't believe in it. But leaving someone like Adithya did, isn't at all appreciable. I saw you kids together and I was happy watching you people trying to love each other. That's why I never forbade you even after hearing your loud boot soles almost every day on my upper floor. Adithya seemed a happier version when you were around, but you are never gonna know if it's a lie. Kid, you are young and beautiful, your future self needs you. Don't cross the ocean for someone who isn't ready to make a jump over the puddles. If he's gonna come back and there's any love left for him, welcome him back, else I better suggest you move on."- He took a pause after saying this at a breath. I never knew Adith's old man was this cool with some scars of youth. Even his words started making me feel guilty for all the things I had said about his restrictive nature over Adith's visitors which were no one except me, and now I knew he never wanted us to improvise. He was actually a support for all those successful days I made with Adith.

"You are right Mr.Sen and I don't know how I can pay my gratitude to you for allowing me near your boy. But for the last thing, did you get anything while cleaning his room after he was gone? Just curious, if there's anything to get into his mind."

Mr.Sen laughed heartily for a few moments. Nikhil looked at me like if he was given a choice; he would surely sword me up right there. The key he found was still peeping from his pocket and he was passing mute sentences while sipping his tea.

"Now I know what you two rats were doing in his room. You really think lady; he has left something for you? I don't think he did, but yes, there were some very normal things I collected as trash from his room. I still have it, maybe. If you want, I can give that to you. If it helps to get over, keep it." and he ambled along the garden and came back with a boxful of crushy things. I admired how he kept his *Adithya*'s things with care after all these days.

"Take it, I was planning to throw it anyway."

He brought a paper box on the table with a cardboard lid and pressed his hand against it. I was planning to open it there, but Nikhil broke the verse, "Open it when you are home, I don't think Mr.Sen and I, any of us is interested to watch you analyzing, even the little dust on it."

He was right. Probably I was gonna do exactly the microanalysis which would bring nothing but disappointment and boredom to them. So, after finishing the last sip of tea, we said bye to the old man and tiptoed towards the gate. He looked a little upset, saying us bye, and his smile wasn't sly enough to cover the inner agony. Maybe after a long time, he enjoyed some young company and letting us leave so early somehow was paining him. Even I was also feeling a thud in my heart while leaving the place I used to come on regular purpose. Adith was the median to connect us all with the same string and when he left, he took those happiness with him. This big house looks so dull and pale without him, maybe Mr.Sen was also thinking the same.

Reaching to the gate, I looked back. The pitiful smile on his face hadn't faded yet and maybe the thoughts of being alone again for all the day, was paining him even more. I scrunched the crisp yellow leaves of his yard and hugged him for the very first time in my life. We both were missing the same person at the same time and the funny thing was, we neither wanted to catch up the void feeling, nor we were ready to confess how amazing life was when Adith was a fragment of it. The hug exchanged the solely painful thoughts which were personal and invisible in the bare naked eyes of other people.

"It's gonna be alright, kid. If life brings him back to you again, tell him I miss him too. And if possible, sometimes, join my lunch table with your friend. I will cook for you kids."

I nodded and smiled with a heavy heart. Never thought this adventure next door would bring so many emotions together. Nikhil was waiting for me outside, and an indulgent smile was lingering in his lips. He was driving the scooter as I was holding the box with both hands and he surprisingly didn't shower a single word he made on my amateur behavior in front of Mr.Sen. His face said he liked Mr.Sen, and, his old and vigorous soul stole Nikhil's heart too. Maybe we can come over again and Nikhil won't make any dissent if I ask him to join.

SPURT OF HOPE

Wake up with my mom's shrieking voice.

"Babyyyyy, you got a mail. Come on down."

My mom's call depends on her mood swings. Among all the names she loves to call me by, *Baby* and *Honey* are the safest ones cause no one can call you *Baby* and greet you with a tight slap. I was trying to cut the mist of my sleepy eyes, as I find brunch as the strongest drug of my day and the dizziness it brings me, I highly doubt that the drug kings like LSD, cocaine, methamphetamine can ever come to its competition. So, I went downstairs strolling like a ghost and my mom handed me over the big envelope and fixed her eyes on me to see what treasure hunt map it contained.

It was from the modeling agency; I registered myself as a model and later responded to their audition call, just to get a free meal on my lazy Sunday. Nikhil missed his class and trained back directly from Kharagpur just to accompany me - more for the meal, less for being my support. Though I never thought myself as the tiniest part as smart and sexy as the other girls in that room, the day went pretty well with some pleasant memories. Away from all the anxiety and stress, Nikhil and I enjoyed a lot. It was for a magazine shoot, so I had to present myself in swimwear in front of the whole crew and the endless criticism in Nikhil's glimpse made me laugh banishing all the negative thoughts away. My parents never support the idea of being half-naked in front of a roomful of judgmental eyes and maintain a flat tummy with the body curves to be on a runway with some fashionable clothes and sometimes almost nothing but lingerie. Most of the families in Bengal don't appreciate the profession of modeling as it deals with a lot of negativity from the society and sometimes some very uncomfortable touches which take really long to get familiar with.

My idea of modeling is much different. Runways and lights create a different world for me. When I watch the Victoria's Secret fashion show, it made me think less about suicides which have been on my mind a lot, lately. Everyday I wake up, I look for a reason to be alive, and pray I never wake up the next morning to put up with myself and look into the mirror to see the human I hate the most in the world. These days I have been thinking about suicides a lot, different forms of it, easiest and the most effective way to make it out. I have searched about it so many times that I have got a call from my local therapist who was asking me to book an appointment to talk about my problems in exchange for eight thousand rupees an hour. No wonder why Indian society is an absolute failure to make their youths live longer before they themselves become their own demons.

I have been following the supermodels since childhood and I have seen some of them were even in a more problematic situation than I was ever in. Their stories somehow make me dream again to accept the flaws and still be prouder of myself than looking for an escape as the easiest way out. So, I don't see anything wrong in craving to be like them despite the reasons my family tries to show me.

The letter was an appreciation card saying,

"Hey Kiyana Mukherjee,

Our judges loved your confidence, style and body language on the runway and we are so happy to let you know that, we want you in our magazine as a new face. You will be shooting with us for the first time as a freelancer, and you will be getting paid for each shoot. If we continue loving your work, you will receive a yearly contract from us. We love you and we are very eager to work with you. The address and the date are given below, and you have to be present there from the first day. For any confusion, please care to buzz us.

You are beautiful."

WWWWWWWHHHHHHHHHHAAAAAAAAAAAAAAAATTTTTTTT!

I am selected as a model!!!! I pinched myself first and when it hurt like hell, I started reading it again. Nope, the letter was still the same and the second read also said that they wanted me in their magazine. The magazine was one of the most expensive and *high-class* ones which you can only find in rich people's drawing rooms. I once dared to buy this magazine to discover what spicy stuff they put in the 'Sex and Wellness' section, but my hideous brother successfully blackmailed me for months and ate free ice creams from my pocket money threatening me every time that he would tell mom that I had read some adult stuffs which I shouldn't.

Though I almost forgot about the audition long ago and was totally deranged into Adith and his mysterious disappearance since I got home, the mail somehow lightened up my heart with some hopes. The hidden desire to be a model slept inside me for years, so when I saw their ad on my Facebook page, I registered through the mail and as usual I forgot the date of audition. The evening before the date, I opened my mail for some reason and I called Nikhil to ask if he was interested in a free lunch in Hyatt cause my mind was still struggling hard to motivate me to attend it rather than lying on the couch and stream Netflix.

Nikhil's voice flamed up in a moment for two reasons. One- there was a completely free five-star lunch and some complimentary drinks for the only one they were allowing to bring as an add-on. Two- there were a whopping number of hot and pretty ladies who were dreaming to get some attention through the limelight of the magazine and for a date as well. Nikhil came back at night, bathed fresh in the very early morning to present himself as a perfect fit for the steamy and luxurious environment. I didn't have ample options though, as they fixed a dress-code with some other restrictions. If Nikhil didn't give his consent, I wouldn't be having this day. He definitely deserves a 'Thanks'.

Mom was still staring at me like a hawk, but I didn't think it was the right time to tell her that I made an audition which she never wanted me to go if she would have been aware of. So, I somehow ignored her saying, "It's nothing important" and went upstairs with slow feet and busted out in joy and started prancing like a puppy after locking up the jamb.

While jumping with hushed feet and measuring my posture in front of the mirror, Adith's box caught my eye. Since I came back home from that morning adventure, I didn't get enough courage to reveal the secrets inside it and the hope of stepping forward into his business was still more exciting than the magazine letter. So, I kept the letter aside, dumped it under a heavy paper weight and opened the box blowing all the teeny-tiny dust cells off.

Mr.Sen probably got the card-board box from any online delivery and he soft-covered the floor with a white paper so that the things could be picked up easily. My all hopes got mortified when I couldn't find anything interesting after all those efforts I put to trespass into his room and got caught for some yummy breakfast from his cool-dude landlord. It wasn't his fault. I couldn't expect him to keep something interesting so that I could follow his footsteps any further unless he wanted me to.

There was a pocket diary where some dates were written without properly mentioning the year and some of them were highlighted with different colors. I also found a famous album of Green Day ``Bullet in a Bible ", which was weird. I never knew Adith was a Music enthusiast, and never saw his whopping admiration towards rock music which made him buy an expensive "Green Day " album which is already available online for free. At the left bottom corner of the record cover, he wrote J.I.A with a black marker in very small unnoticeable letters. I knew it was his hand-writing cause the patterns he put in vowels is pretty rare in our generation of sadist kids. But after thinking about uniting skies, I couldn't find any appropriate whole words for J.I.A that could represent anything about him. Even Alexa also misled me with some JIA disease that had absolutely no reference with the album or the person I was fixing my thoughts on.

Therefore I spent my one hour in a nutshell and still couldn't remember if those highlighted dates ever involved me. Some of the dates were yet to come as there were some years written with the last two digits just in case I assumed it right. But what about those? Winter dates were marked in red and summer dates were marked in blue. Even though the color codes probably meant something, my stupid brain wasn't intellectual enough to process any proper significance, and after some thoughtful hours with failure, a severe indolence engulfed my will. So, I started randomly fanning with the diary and saw a little piece of folded paper fell down on my feet. I took it up within seconds and unfolded with busy hands. The small piece of paper said, "Adithya & K" ,and there was nothing else. Again it was his own hand-writing and I didn't know if the K was anyone but me. And unless I am getting him in my room, making him sit in front of me with his hands cross-folded, there's no confrontation and confirmation of the signs he left as these complicated metaphors.

I folded it again and kept it as it was hugging the diary. After sitting longer in the chair, my back started hurting and it actually reminded me that in a long time, I trivialized my table as a good place to write like the way I used to, especially when my mind was sputtered and overthinking with shitty ideas.

I noted down the dates in my writing pad, did some quick stretches to get rid of the small pains, and invaded my pillows to get some lazy time reading the mail again and again. The prologue of being happy was no longer making me dance leaps and bounds when I noticed the location was in another city. They were organizing the shoot in Delhi and if I wanted to make it up to them, I had to tell my parents. I just couldn't get a flight in the morning, did the shoot and returned back in the evening. They needed to be supportive enough to send me there to get my work done and if they said "no", my whole overwhelming glee would be screwed.

At this moment, I had two people to call for convincing my parents effectively- Kanishk and Nikhil. But Nikhil was the safest option as he would at least pick up my call without any excuse. For Kanishk, if it's his study hours, he would hardly pretend to notice.

My brother Kanishk - an IIT Bombay Computer Science grad, currently on his way to put a new feather on his crown by clearing UPSC after one very close-cut failed attempt. From childhood, growing up with a school and then college topper wasn't any less than a vengeance, and his ignorance towards me for being not-up-to-the-mark as he does, always ate me up from inside. My relatives used to visit us and they could hardly get time to ask about me after listening up all the amazing victories my brother made as a kid ahead of his age. He cleared JEE with AIR 6, and he forcefully made me do all the cutting from the newspapers who wrote flattering articles on him. Then he left home and completed four years in Bombay and got a job in San Francisco and I finally got some relief of living a life without his physical presence. But it was my mom who caught almost every health problem overthinking about her son, and dad wasn't also supporting him to stay abroad after listening to the problems he was facing there, due to lack of adjustment skills.

It was both my parent's idea to convince him for UPSC, and finally he started preparing from there. Therefore, he came back to Delhi when his company granted his transfer and he got a better environment there in my aunt's house. My aunt is a divorced and childless lady, and she enthusiastically accepted Kanishk to stay over and till now, she is dwelling with that piece of crap. Last year, he cleared the mains but got stuck in the interviews. Maybe that was the first time he got some taste of reality. Consecutive conquests made him an arrogant lad, and that was the first time I saw him being a little polite to me. I was happy that he was actually learning some social skills rather than hooking up with some random chicks, and leaving them high and dry when he was bored. But his silence approached some wretched feeling in me too. Inside the crowd of all the hatred and the bad days he caused me, somehow I am terribly proud of Kanishk and at the end of the day, that love and admiration for him is still alive no matter how many times he scrounged my pocket money over stupid excuses.

Nikhil was probably in his room when I called him, enjoying his snack or masturbating in the short intervals between the classes. The schedule of IIT Kharagpur is pretty tight with regular classes and extracurricular activities, so he hardly gets time to be responsive to my calls in the daytime. IIT KGP was always his dream college, but when the dream touches reality, you have to accept the consequences that come along with the perks and fulfillment. But I never heard him complaining about the strict life he got there after always being cared, loved and pampered at his house 24x7. He is a boy of adjustments and compromises unlike Kanishk who used to be a loner for his whole first year of college and call mom almost fifty times a day to elaborate how fucking hard life was, as he had to do all the small chip chops on his own.

"Hey Kenny, what's up?"

"You are free now? I have some news."

"Yah, next class in an hour, I think you can finish your news within."

"Yah, listen, you remember that we went to an audition in Hyatt Regency and you stole my free drink…"

"I didn't steal it; I took it for your good. Those sugary drinks can make you fat. It's better not to… but what about that?"

"I made the audition and they want me for their magazine……..in Delhi…"

"Whhhhhhhhhhhhhaaaaaatttt? Why the hell on earth do they want your stupid face on their magazine?"

"Shut up! I got the mail in the morning, but the thing is, the shoot is in Delhi. So, you have to convince my parents to grant me the trip."

Nikhil was probably chewing something, and after finishing a mouthful, he calmly said, "So, you are again putting the gun on my shoulder, huh! Let me think about all the previous favors you did to me, and if those are substantial enough, I will try to make it."

"Nik, please, the date is in the next month. If I am going, I have to prepare myself accordingly. It's not the time for joke."

"Who said I am joking? And you are well-aware that your parents are absolutely against the modeling industry. So, even if I say "yes", getting a "yes" from them won't be an easy one. Have you tried telling Kanishk, he stays in Delhi? You can stay with him."

"If I request him, he will first ask a million questions just to say "no" afterwards."

"He's a funny guy, I love him."- Nikhil laughed like there's nothing serious.

"Are you gonna do it or not? I am losing my mind now."

"If you need a favor, you say"Please "."

There was some gravely silence for two minutes. The only sound of Nikhil's crisps was crackling my ears, and with time, he was intentionally chewing more loudly to make my ear nerves shiver.

"Enough, stop chewing like a freak, and please tell my parents, please. I really want to do it."

"Let me think till the evening. If I find plausible points to support you, I will see. Now, I have classes, I gotta run."

He cut the phone putting me in a question mark, and I had to wait till the night to know if he had made up his mind anyhow.

After lunch, I was feeling a little bit dizzy while leaning on my pillow and trying to go through the chapter of Advance Java. It's on my college syllabus and as usual I was never one of those brilliant minds who find programming fascinating. Though Adith was a commerce grad, he had some impressive grip on programming. When I used to sneak into Mr.Sen's house, the first thing Adith used to do was to check my bag if I bought any of my computer books. Computer science was never on my priority list, but after the board's results, it was Kanishk's idea to baffle my head into this subject just because of his expertise in it. Though I never got any proper help from him to get rid of the hatred I had for programming, he never missed a chance to lecture on my disabilities to learn this subject effectively.

After finishing first few pages, I felt even more bored than I was before and was flipping the pages blankly to kill the dizziness. But according to me, textbooks are more powerful than lullabies and I am always just a humble disciple of its magical power to make people sleep. So, my dizziness occupied my nerves even more intensely, and soon, the little fonts of the book started getting blurred in my vision. But between the war of flowing with the nerves or waking myself up for finishing the chapter, a small blurry line at the very bottom corner in one of the pages made me stand through my pheromones. It was Adith's handwriting and I remember he wrote it on my notebook as his house Wi-Fi was troubling him that day and he wanted me to send a draft mail for his tuition. Later he didn't need it anymore and I absolutely forgot to connect him through the mail. The id already got faded with time, but it was still readable. I ran over my pencil to dig it up clean and now I could read the id more prominently. "AdithyaKMukherjee02@gmail.com"- he loved my surname more than I did and this was the only holy place he got to reconstruct it with his name. 02 stands for my birthday on 2nd August, and the K is for my name. I wasn't aware about his other mail ids and I never cared to find any. He created this one, so that I could send him my study materials or movie links or any interesting thing that I think might interest him.

All these days of witch-hunting and listening to those 'You-have-dialed-a-wrong-number' IVR tones, I totally forgot about mailing him as a last pebble of hope. So, I quickly dragged down my laptop, set it up comfortably on my lap after clearing all the unwanted dust, and started writing, clicking on the compose button.

To: <u>AdithyaKMukherjee02@gmail.com</u>

From: <u>KennyMukherjee02@gmail.com</u>

Subject: A Mail Of Hope

I know it's a very dumb idea to look for you when you want to ghost yourself intentionally, but when the mail id popped up in front of me somehow, I thought of writing this to you as a last twist of communication.

Last Wednesday, it rained heavily. It rained in whites, blurring the visions of the nearest things; it rained like the clouds are crushing through the hills and showering to rinse off all the grieves; merely it rained like you always wanted. Monsoon is about to start so does the pain of all your memories of us. I wonder if you remember me the same way I do, when it rains. I wonder if you also stare at the ceiling in your lazy hours, cherish those moments we spent together and mourn for the void I feel every night. Do these distances and longings ever weigh you down? Or you've got someone precious enough to fall for your smiles every day. I wonder if you smile the same way, spreading your lips to the most, creasing your eyes underneath. Can she read your eyes like me? Does she touch your naked soul where there's no falling or escape? Is she a good listener? Does she wake up next to you and lean on your chest until it's the time to go?

After all these months, your voice, your touch, your nostalgia are still alive in me. I wonder if we ever meet again, will your hug still feel the same! Will you still smell like petrichor melts with some expensive eau-de-cologne?

I recall those days when you used to lay on bed and I used to prance all over the room in your baggy T-shirt to make you laugh with my stupid moves. I still admire how the silence in the room never made us uncomfortable and how amazingly you could read my mind even if the words fell out differently.

I wonder if it's the advent of monsoon too, where you are right now. Do you still adore the rain like the way you used to or it has become just the muddy fields and moisty crossroads for you?

Even though I know you gave up on me a long ago and trying to get you back is nothing but a lost cause, I will still hope for you to come back, for me, to let me touch your face again and ask you the same question I have been asking myself every day, "Why even in a million times, inside those billions changing faces, into a world of ungrateful people, why? Why wouldn't you ever choose me? Where, since I met you, I never doubted for a second that you are my only ever and after!"

I remember your eyes the last day I saw you. You wanted me to stay a little more, you wanted me to be your night, for looking at our future, together. Your eyes were overwhelming with affection. Not for a single second I thought that was a lie. I just wanted a few moments, to sit and talk, to make you aware how deadly you make me feel when you talk about leaving, and here we are today, when I have actually spent almost a year without you. I hate myself more than I do you. I hate how you still make me as crazy as before, I hate how everything still feels the same, and how I come up with newer excuses to hurt myself everyday.

Be safe where you are and where you would be next, and if you ever make mind to come back or think about the girl you left behind, remember the afternoons we spent, making promises under the same sky; remember the way I never tried to learn to live alone; remember all the love you swirled up in my heart which is still alive in me every moment, every day; remember there's always a door open for you to come back and diffuse inside my entity. I am not finished loving you, and I won't ever do. You are my forever, Adith.

I don't know how and why I still love you so bad and how I kill my existence everyday by dissolving you inside me. I don't want to love you anymore, I can't keep being alive like this. I want to be free from the grief you cause me every night. I want to be happy as a normal 20 year old. Please Adith, please come, and help me erase you from my life.

I stopped. Writing down your emotions on a computer screen isn't always a cinch to do, especially when you know there won't be any reply and maybe the recipient will never gonna open your mail. So, I overthought all the excuses for not sending the mail, but still someone in my mind murmured, "What if he is waiting for some signs from you! What if he loves the mail and sends a reply! What if…"

There's always an *if* after what. But what if I send the mail and see what happens next. For the worst case, he won't even open it or he will delete it after seeing my mail id. So, finally I put all the courage together and clicked the send button after rechecking the spellings.

Switching off my notebook, I came back to my bed and looked through the window. It was an almost-monsoon evening, and the sky was colored in egg-yolk-yellow. Though it didn't rain for two days, the hypnotic cool breeze was bringing the essence of the upcoming monsoon, cooling down the pitch-melting humidity of Kolkata.

Through the window, I saw dad crossing the yard hanging his office bag on the left hand, which was weird cause he mostly comes home at or after 9 p.m. It was 5:50 only, and his coming back in an early hour made me a bit curious. I was thinking of going downstairs to ask about his health, then I heard the call, "Kenny, come downstairs, we need to talk."

"We need to talk" is a universal preface of something really destructive. It can be a break-up, bad news, a rejection and many more that can make your veins crush through all the blood. So, my heart skipped a beat when I started assuming what kind of things I could receive when I went downstairs.

I saw mom and dad were sitting at the dining table silently fixing their eyes on me as long as it took me to come to the table. Dad was switching his eyes over the phone sometimes, but I know my mom very well. Her face was calm, slightly bothered and filled with annoyance. I have been familiar with this face since childhood for every time I did something that I wasn't supposed to do. Even after all these years, I am not even a little less scared of this face than I used to.

"Sit down."- My mom ordered in a non-ordering tone.

I sat down like the most obedient child on earth and my nerves were about to declare a shutdown. For one moment, I got a flashback of all the shady stuffs I had done and in the worst case what would be the final conclusion if my parents got to know them!

"Kenny, you never told us you are interested in modeling and you are putting serious thoughts on it."

Thank god! It's about the audition, not about something more undercover.

"Papa, I just went there casually; to see how things happen. I had no intention to make it. I was just happy when I got the mail and I just told Nikhil that I made it. He was there with me, that's why…"

"It's funny how you think we are the worst decision makers and somehow you convinced Nik to accompany you with these stupid ideas."

I put my face down in guilt.

"Raya, let her talk. Kenny, don't you trust us?"

"Where does that come from? Of course, I trust you."

"Then why didn't you tell us or ask for permission before going to an audition."

"I thought you guys were not gonna let me go."

"And why do you think that?"

"Cause you don't like me being myself. You want me to be a successful man like Kanishk."

My answer might get them into some serious realization. All these years of constant comparisons and the burden of judgments for *why two siblings are so different-* made me nothing but feeling like a worthless. Every time I tried to give my best, I ended up being disheartened and resentful cause my brother was always better than my best. The strict margin of not being a brilliant mind like him weighed me down each and every day. Even when I started to accept myself behind all those comparisons, no one actually bothered to care about my feelings. From the neighbors to our relatives, my all good was always less than the perfection of my brother and some of them were highly fascinated about how I was not even a little jealous like the way they expected me to be, after all these depreciation they always had crafted on my mind.

"What's the problem with you? Are you losing your mind? You think you can be a star posing at the front page of Grazia magazine? They are going to make your career up like any millionaire model? Come down to reality. There will be no future unless you have a good educational background and stop wasting your time on these useless things."-Mom's voice just heated up.

"Ain't I already useless, Mom?"

"Oh now you are talking over me. Who is chewing your brain to be this arrogant? Is this the college effect?"

I could cry but I chose not to. All these years, I wasted my tears for all the criticism and ignorance I got from my *so called* relatives, for whom my efforts were never enough to make me up-to-the-mark and now it's very normal that my parents aren't gonna listen to me just because the number of achievements I have in my bag is zero. So, I chose silence rather than making them realize how crap I had always felt for being a good-for-nothing to them, and never been appreciated for being a different entity with a humble soul that Kanishk never had.

"Raya, Raya, please let her talk. Kenny, we are here to listen. I think we have engraved some misunderstanding in your heart. It's totally our fault, but it's yet not too late to talk. I will listen to you, Ma. Whatever is in your mind please talk it out."

Even after sulking over them all these years, deep down dad's words comforted me. Somehow I felt that at least he would listen to me for the first time in my whole life. Maybe he would be a hope I can convince that not everyone wants to be a college topper or a successful officer, some want to fly high enough to be an outlaw for the society. I no longer wanted to hurt my spine or invite more backaches for running a simple Java program from 9 to 5 just because that stuff didn't get into my brain or excite my neurons. If I were physically, and financially independent, I would probably build a house, get a dog and stay there away from these city commotions and politics. Or I would probably make Adith stay with me for an apparent era of *happily ever after*. Though this phase is a lie and there's no *happy, ever* and *after*, but with the right person, even the wrong time can also start feeling right. It's not about the day or the evening or the middle of the night, it's about the existences, the feelings you grow, the moments you evolve, the warmth you share and the love that combines your soul to the universe. It's never about how much money or how many degrees you can collect in your life, but the integrity that actually differentiates you from a machine.

But the path of being independent always crosses through the streets of thrones through the degrees and the points. You can be the wisest person in the room and still be umpired with the CGPA points you have successfully stolen from your examination hall. Nobody gives a fuck if you have ungodly abilities to solve calculus unless you have a goddamn degree to prove it on paper. World is unfair, my friend.

"Papa, I want to do it, I want to give it a try. I seriously do."- I broke the silence as it was maiming me.

Dad nodded his head positively and said, "I believe you can do it. If it makes you happy, you can go. I will tell Kanishk to receive you from the airport and stay there in your aunt's house as long as you need. If I can manage time, I will be there to cheer you up."

Mom didn't say anything; she just looked at dad with a little hope. I didn't know this face for me. Hopes were the section where only Kanishk had the access. I never saw them hoping on me. It was a whole new thing.

It was like hearing something scripted that I always wanted them to say. Maybe dad is right. It's yet not too late, I still have time to fix these broken pieces of puzzles of the relationship with my family. Maybe it was partially my fault too that I never let them know how I felt. Maybe there's still something left that yet hasn't started to wane.

THE MONSOON WORTH WAITING FOR

It's raining outside. It started with some drizzles and now the raindrops are even dominating the thunder roars. Adith is lying beside me, so close that I can hear the silence of his breaths. It's one O'clock at night. He's peacefully asleep and the serenity in his face is some unearthly thing that wiped away all the grudges I kept on holding. The aroma of his after-shave lotion massifies the whole room with the pleasure of breathing. I probably can forget people's faces after a long detachment, but in no situation, I can forget how they smell. I have the power to signify their smell, even if it takes a decade to see those familiar faces again. Just that way, my olfactory neurons were always sensitive to his presence. Even a lot of times, when I smelt something relatively familiar, I rushed to it, stayed there for a bit and prayed to stop there forever. But I never chased the smell to keep it in my room. I let it be a complete mystery, to be waiting for it, to be sudden, to be worth breathing, every little particle, when met again.

A sleepy face is the purest, may not the person be, but whatever life gives you back at the moment, and whenever it's this much precious, I can't help but reversing it. I took my face closer to him, to breathe him with every little detail. His presence was maddening, everything I ever craved, and of course never thought of getting in real.

'What are you, Adith? A magic'

The monsoon has arrived. Raining these days is pretty normal, but if you have an artistic heart, no monsoon will ever leave you alone. It will play a cadenza if you put little credence in its superiority to paint your heart. I am always a pluviophile, so does Adith. We enjoy the rain and its aftermath to the sky. Though I didn't get enough monsoons to spend with him, whenever it rains I see him more like an old soul than he actually is. For me, monsoon is way more appealing than perspiring summer, and chilly-willy winter. I think there wouldn't be any romance genre without monsoon; maybe people would've found arts overrated without it. Maybe no artist would be born unless it started pouring from the sky making their pens mightier with thoughts.

After a five-hours-long nap, I finally got out of bed and lit up a candle. Power lights kill resilience. And it's too late to light up the LEDs and sit beside the window with a cup of coffee. Also, I don't want to wake Adith up as he didn't get a bit of rest since I got here. After receiving me from the airport, and doing all the groceries, he did the cooking, cleaning all by himself. My extreme inefficiency in house work resisted me from helping him in fear of overdoing his perfection. He cooked most of the foods I possibly love and arranged a textbook dining with the flowers and drinks. His efforts to make our day exceptional and unforgettable, make me a lot more content than the actual foods and drinks. I never thought I would receive a welcome like this, even after contemplating all the possibilities of him forgetting me so far.

In the little flame of the candle, the room looks even bigger and holier than I thought. The thunder roars accompanied with heavy showers will seemingly going to end the supremacy of the bird chirps. From today, the rainy season is taking over and there will be more rumbles and dark clouds rather than the soft songs of the morning bird. For me, the rainy winds are the moral longings; like you desire for a warm hand while crossing a busy road, a hug when your world is falling apart, a lover when your heart is sculpting some nostalgia of romanticism away from your physical cravings; just like that, the rainy winds can be softer than a moonlit night.

I lean on the cotton curtains and shape myself against the wall to admire the show of lights and shower outside. If you listen to it silently, the lightning will no longer scare you, rather it will make things visible in a different way that will make you think about its existence once again. Adith is still asleep, and only the candle light is contributing some glow on his face. Before today, I had never been so appreciative of the beauty of little things. The smell of new soil soaked in rain, the greener-than-the-green glow in the groves, the beauty of your favorite face in the dimmest light, they are all feeling so wholesome to me. Our room is somehow coinciding with the flow of the universe. I can't describe the mundanity and spirituality it possesses away from the concrete hearts of the city folks.

I go back to bed and move my face closer enough to draw a kiss on his forehead. He is warm, innocent and beautiful. My kiss woke him up and his sleep-drenched voice felt like some honey-shower to my ears.

"You didn't sleep?"

I smiled like a fool and said, "Just got up a few minutes ago, and was planning to spend the rest of the night staring at your face."

Adith smiled even brighter.

"That's definitely not a good idea; you will bore yourself to sleep."

"I certainly not, sir. But why do you wake up this early? You had a tiring day, Adith. Go, sleep."

"What if I implicate your idea of spending the night!"

"Still old puns, huh? You haven't changed a bit, do you?"

"My lady loves the old soul, so why is there anything to change? By the way, I still can't believe Kanishk allowed you to stay with me. I think he has changed a lot."

"He's trying to be a lesser asshole with me, nothing else. I already switched off my phone, else he wouldn't let me sleep with random calls."

"I can't blame him though. Allowing your sister to stay with a pervert who fucking cheated on her and left mysteriously, isn't a very easy-going decision. Not every brother let their sisters be this independent. He did. Don't blame him."

"Adith, shut up. I never thought of you as a pervert, I can never do. You left for your own reasons and maybe I didn't give you enough grounds to stay. I never blame you for any of that. If I did, we would probably not be having this day. Kanishk was always mean to me. Now, I am just giving him an opportunity to be a good brother. I hope he works on it."

"Aren't you angry? Don't you feel like writing my name on a piece of paper and setting it on fire? Why Kenny? Why are you so merciful?"- He supports his head to his left arm, bringing his face nearer to mine.

"I think you already know my answer. But when you have the realization, why did you leave?"

"I had to."- He moved his face towards the ceiling, probably was trying to ignore my eyes.

"Why?"

"I don't know. It's hard to explain. I want to let you stay with me, but I can't. I don't know how I get myself into this dilemma, Kenny. You are still a child to me. I will tell you everything when it is the right time."

"What if your right time takes me to the grave?"

"Don't talk to me like that. Come on, come under the blanket. The night is getting colder."

I silently followed his words and he widely spread the blanket over my long legs to cover me up from the moisty winds. His touch felt like that little flame of light flickering from any distant stranger's lantern, that keeps a lost soldier hopeful on the deserted streets at the darkest night on earth. I craved for this touch in my every night of disappointment and cursed myself to sleep for imagining some impossible world of pleasure that was probably never going to happen. I missed him, I missed him, I missed him. Oh god! How badly I missed everything about him.

It's the time we let the sky whine for us. All the storms I never allowed to erode by time, kept the fire alive inside my heart. I had trucks of questions lumped in my throat, but I chose silence as a satisfying answer for everything. Unless he thinks it's the right time for me to know, he's never gonna open up. He can probably be a drug dealer, or a sleeper cell, an international spy or a wizard or anything that I can't possibly think of, but none of these identities can ever change my love for him. When I am gonna know, I am gonna know. Before that, I don't think it's a spicy topic to keep the debates on.

"Adith, did you miss me?"

I was lying on his chest like I used to and he was combing my hair with his fingers. This is the most non-sexual way of fulfilling me, the holiest desire my heart can always wrench for.

"Did you leave any choice not to?"

"Then why didn't you even try to contact? You just left me in a deep sea with a bunch of '*Why*'s. You didn't reply to my mail, you erased all your contacts, there's no note, nothing, and I can't ask you why. Have you ever thought how I felt all these days?"

Adith was silent, his fingers didn't stop combing my hair and all I could hear was more and more rumbling of thunder.

"Adith, you listening to me?"- I broke the silence as there was no reply from his side.

"Kenny, let's cut the mist. I am really sorry for whatever damage I've done to you and to be very honest; leaving you right there ripped my heart apart. I am not here to convince you to stay with me or to accept my innocence, I know I am not; but there's something I can't tell. And lurking from you all the time is the worst thing that has scrounged my good night's sleep."- He stopped for a minute. Then he went up straight and held both my hands gently to make me get up nearer to his lap. He kept his head down for a bit and then continued, "Do you think leaving you was just a game for me? I didn't burn any less than you did. The difference is you got people to express your feelings; I was dying on my own. When I got your mail, it was the only happiness that kept me alive. I used to read it every day before bed, and answer all your queries on my own. I just wish that you will hear me one day, and I could tell you everything you want to know. It wasn't supposed to happen. I tried to set you free that day, I tried to forget every single thing we had, but I couldn't. You are everywhere, in my every day, at my every moment. Every time I looked at something beautiful it reminded me of you. Even if I eat outside, I try to avoid the dessert section. I remember your craziness over desserts and it almost kills me to see someone else admiring it the same way. The loneliness was supposed to be fun, but it's you, Kenny. Your memories never let me be alone, even at my toughest. Why? Why didn't you just forget about me like a nightmare? Why didn't you hate me enough to bury the memories with me? Why does your mail still hit my inbox when I never planned to reply? Why the prettiest orchard still smells like your hair? Why do your memories still don't let me sleep at night? I was going to be okay after you, but why didn't you let me be?"

Maybe he wasn't finished with his form of grievances, but I pulled him against my chest so that if there's any male emotion left, dying to come out, it would better be absorbed in me. I didn't know if he was being the truest version of him or it was just a fallback for the moment, but I trusted him. All my instincts were pushing me through the edges to believe him with everything. The moments weren't lying, so were my intentions. All these days, I waited for a night like this, to denude our souls, and talk about every feeling we were scared to convey.

"It's alright, we are together now. Look! How happy we are right now. Will you still keep complaining?"- I was rubbing my hand gently on his back and his face was busy digging deep inside my soft breasts to reach the warmth of my heart.

What is left to say now? What could I possibly ask to summon his integrity? He left no space to unlove him.

"Kenny!"- He lifted up his face.

"Yah"

"If we ever get a chance………………..will you stay with me?"

"For a thousand lifetimes, in a million worlds of possibilities, I would find you with every approachable version of me. Adith, I can't lose you at any cost. Doesn't matter if you choose to stay with me or not, I will choose you in every universe, every day, every moment my senses keep me alive. You are the one I have been looking for all my life, Adith. You are my thing; only my thing."- I let ourselves melt into one.

The howling of the clouds somehow concurred with the restlessness of our heart. His tired physique is resting on me, and the silence of the room is healing our lamentations. This is the monsoon worth waiting for. This is the monsoon worth living a thousand lives. Just me and him.

KANISHK & LIFE

"Got your tickets?"

"Yup!"

"Where's your water bottle? Hanky? You got your hanky?"

"Did you tell your son not to kill me there?"

"What's wrong with you? Why are you always in a bad mood?"

"You're asking these silly questions in spite of knowing all these are available in my flight!"

"When you become a mom, you will understand the value of these words."

"Yes, I will. My cab is here, I have to go."

Dad was waiting in the cab and it was honking repeatedly as my voice couldn't reach them to confirm I was on the way. Before leaving for a few days for the first time in life, she kissed me endlessly on cheeks, forehead, and my jawline. She was upset. I saw it on her face. At least I mattered to her and that was the biggest piece of cake I was taking with me. I kissed her back too, and already started feeling the bulging insecurities of the upcoming events. The destination was unsure, and the instincts weren't usual. The path I was on was a whole new world for me. I was in a flight, all by myself, ignoring the flight mates like a blurry background in a portrait. Dad left from outside, and kissed me bye from there. Nikhil couldn't manage a holiday from the college and I insisted him not to. Traveling all the way just to say Goodbye felt like a luxury to me. The distances were insane and the purpose wasn't worth the effort. I got a window seat at one request and that was a huge relief to avoid interacting with any over-enthusiastic co-passenger by never turning my face on them from the view outside my window.

For the first few moments, I felt like crying, but I couldn't let it out. I was afraid that my sobs could catch some unwanted attention and that might create a mess. My mind was flooding with some random thoughts of going back home and lying on my bed like forever. For some moments, I didn't wanna go anywhere- to the opportunities, in a new city, in a new failure! I wanted to stay home- stay until my bones start growing green leaves on it. I didn't know how Kanishk would react to my staying with him after all these years of severe detachment and huddling grudges. And my biggest fear was to make things worse as we both were adults and adults never say *sorry* easily.

The flight was too fast to complete my short downloaded Spotify playlist. I came to the waiting room with a tiring mind and weighty lashes - looking for a familiar face to lap me up from the world of unknown, smart people and drop me off in a bed of peace. I wanted a roomful of me, my solitude, Kalsea Ballerini in my playlist and a black coffee probably. I hate crowds, people and everything that is loud. I never wanted to hear what kind of midlife crisis my co-passenger was facing through his loud and excited phone calls with his distant wife. My face already got dead when the kids started running everywhere and sometimes crashing with my stroller that collided with my knee for a pretty fair amount of time. And I was even more surprised to see their moms were just chilling and gossiping with each other without fixing them in one spot.

When the time fudged enough with disgust, I thought I could take no more. I was not made for this chaos. It would be better if I would just stay home and do nothing until the god of death decided to come along and scrounge me from the earthly senses.

I was just thinking about getting up and finding my way to aunt's place, I saw Kanishk's face- talking over the phone by holding it in one hand and waving towards me to reach him with another. Though mom said Kanishk would come to pick me, I never thought he would actually gonna show up. I didn't save his new number in my phone and I believed he did the same. So, there was no straight way of connecting him. Seeing him after an era, in a situation, from where I was dying to elude, felt pretty safe. He wasn't a high-school boy anymore; he was a 6 ft 2 tall, handsome and grown-up guy. I had to admit that he had grown as an unscriptedly handsome man with trimmed beard and ice-cold eyes. We both have mom's eyes and this way we are even. Apart from that, he is just 4 inches taller than me with a big brain and a mean heart.

I reached him with slow feet, and heard him confirming over phone that he finally got me. Then he handed it over and I heard the worried voice of mom who got some relief after hearing me good. Kanishk took one of my strollers and remained silent while walking towards the gate until I started.

"You could have called me, what if I was….."

"I don't have your number."- He didn't let me finish.

"Fair enough, but what if I wasn't in the waiting room!"

"That would be your fault. I was told to pick you up from there, not to do a manhunt."

His words were enough to make me feel miserable for meeting him after so long. But this was the behavior I was expecting as a welcome gift, so nothing from him made me feel that bad.

"I didn't expect a pretty face though. You used to be an average kid when I saw you last. You are working out, huh?"- At least he called me pretty- that's what I picked from those lines.

"For a year now."

"Good for you. You remember, you used to be the weirdest kid in school. What magic potion you had to outgrow from that nerdy face to this...!!!!!"

Then he came closer and stopped to get a good stare at me. Even after all those years, his creepy condemnatory mind didn't change at all.

"What's your problem, Kanishk? This is how you say hi to your sister? What's wrong with you?"

"What's wrong with me? You came down here to destroy my peace in life and you are asking what's wrong with me? Kenny, I don't like to be surrounded with people or interacting with them by formalities. I don't have social skills, so don't expect me to be dramatic like your new-age fake people. Just mind your own business, and I will mind mine, so there's no collision."

But there's a thin line between being dramatic and caring, I hope you never know, Kanishk- I didn't say it out loud, I mumbled. From the first interaction, I perfectly understood that- the more we spoke, the worse the relationship would become. So, silence was the safest option to survive those days with him.

In my aunt's house, I got a pretty warm welcome. She prepared all the things I loved and seeing the table decorated finely with all those, my ab lines already started melting down. Her happy face consoled my insolvent heart a little bit and the warmth of the place made me feel light.

At night, I crawled to Kanishk's room and knocked twice after keeping my fist away from the door and taking half an hour to assume how he would gonna react to see me at his door at that time.

He opened the door quietly and looked straight into my eyes with overwhelming revulsion. If I were a kid, my heart would have frozen to death to the lightning of rage he was throwing at me, but anything that came from him was no longer as scary as before. For me, he was just an arrogant sod spoiled by the idea of hostile inhumanity. He was never a brother. He was an ideal son, student, maybe a friend, a topper and many more, but not a brother! It would be much better if we weren't siblings, not even closer to anything like blood relatives. I would rather prefer being unborn than being his sister. We would have been the best if stayed strangers.

"What do you want?"

"I am confused about the address they gave me. Thought of asking you just in case you know how to reach!"

He kept his eyes straight on me for a few seconds, and then slowly lowered them to check the address blinking on my phone screen. It looked like that place wasn't unfamiliar to him and now he had to pass the hurdle to direct me in.

"I will book a cab tomorrow, and I hope you won't disturb me at night any further."

He got the affirmation from my expression, so it was not a very hard task for him to slam the door on my face without telling me to leave directly. Years passed, but somehow he managed to stay the same with me – cold-hearted and brutal. I was just too indolent to figure out *WHY?*

The next day I woke up early in the morning, got ready for the voyage I was hailed down here for. Kanishk is always an early riser, so he booked the cab and told aunt to call her up when the event would end. I reached there, posed in front of the camera in multiple costumes and hair styles and realized that I was actually enjoying doing them. I didn't even notice when the morning sun vanished in the sore, and the cloudy darkness of the night came without catching my attention, not even for once. After a long time, I felt like my caged spirit finally set free. I didn't care about the ultimatum, whether I would be one of their final faces or not. I just enjoyed the spotlight and that was all that mattered to me. After the audition ended, one of the judges came to me, said she saw a fire within, and there were chances that I would be something someday. As she was a famous lady in her profession, I couldn't possibly say she had any other intention. So, I stayed with her for a few moments then came outside to call my aunt, and got home.

September in Delhi was pretty hot and rainy sometimes. The evening stretched long to overrule the night. I didn't feel like going home that early. The clock struck 7:30 and the roads got busier every minute. I had a little money in my pocket, so I came to the footbridge to have tea and to ear those Delhite conversions from the crowd. The tea was nice. Not too good, not too bad; just nice! And how amazing it felt not to be chased by the chances of getting some familiar faces around! A new city, an unknown lane, with a pack of uninterested strangers who didn't even look at me once. I started loving the crowd for not counting me in the existence. I never enjoyed indifference so briefly. My mind was at a peace for not being seen or heard. I loved the invisibility they gifted me.

I strolled down to the end of the footbridge where it fell over on a road. It wasn't crowded but it wasn't empty either. People were scattered into places- some were jostling at a snack-shop, others were on their way. Nobody was looking at any way other than their own businesses.

I sat down on a concrete pipe that was lying lonely at the end of the lane. My heels curled up on the streets trying to draw a line as this was the only thing rounding around my head. Sometimes I was checking my phone, trying to look busy with those empty apps and notifications which started getting very usual with my boring life. Therefore I was free for those moments, free for being void, sitting there and doing nothing. These days, people never get time to lie on bed empty-headed. I got that opportunity. I was lucky.

Suddenly, in the middle of nowhere I felt a hunch of discomfort; something very odd - like someone was staring at me straight, without blinking their eyes. That was a side vision, so I turned my face to the left and the face I saw buried me to the grave after overkilling my soul a million times. It was a tall, handsome gentleman in a dusky sweatshirt where the off colors were making him unworthy of catching attention in such a dark evening of an almost-deserted lane. It was Adithya; to be more familiar, Adith - to whom I surrendered not once, not twice; over a million times like that time itself. He was just a couple of hands away from me - restless, sore and awestruck. He was probably as shaken as I was; at least his blurry presence was saying so. In a moment, he came so close that I could easily notice the wrinkles of both surprise and shock in his face. Moreover that was the time I realized he wasn't looking at me; he was looking into me, observing and trying to assume if there was any shade of him still left by which he could pass through and rip me off again. It was merely my imagination about what I felt after seeing him there, unplanned, unexpectedly after a year. I didn't know if my thoughts were valid or I was just seeking excuses to rescue myself from falling for him again.

For a few moments, we both didn't know what to do. For a few seconds, I thought I should run; run until I saw my existence craving for him no longer. But in my world, there was no place without him at all. I was trapped again. But this time, there was a little more maturity to stand against the falls, to take things like adults. So, I proceeded a little and heard him speaking first.

"Kenny!"

I smirked.

"What are you doing here?"

"Minding my own business, probably."- I didn't ask about his well-being either. I know that was rude, but I had no choice than to do this for pushing him back. He was my heartlocker and I didn't want to be in the same place I was in, a year ago. Maybe my love for him never expired or maybe I was that same freak as before, but one thing I realized in the whole year of pain was that not all the loves need the same way of expression. Some loves are dangerous like mine. It almost got me killed. So, it was safer to love him from a distance. Less physical but the same way sensitive.

"Yah, that's great. Ummm! I should probably get going."

I nodded.

I saw him hesitating to say something further. I needed him to go, but I wanted him to kiss me first. I wanted the kiss be so intense and wild that every spirit down the lane would stop and stare. But it wouldn't be just a kiss. It would be a wildfire wrapped in a magic, which might take me back to where I started. It would be the cycle of destruction again. I was young, wild and desperate. One touch in my frozen lake of desires, and I am fire again. And that fire wouldn't probably go away without flurrying my ashes in the wind. So, I let him slip away from my sight.

The empty street became emptier and so did my heart. My phone was in my hand and it would probably be the best idea if I had called my aunt to book a cab for me. But I didn't and I chose to stay there pointlessly. The flashback of real moments actually started hitting me then. The moment I was waiting for all these days, was there and I just let it pass away. I remembered all the questions I prepared for him if I ever met him again by the rules of destiny, and I couldn't ask any of them. I was too busy to ignore him that I almost forgot, I had business to close with him. At least I should've asked why he did what he did, or where he had been all these days, cutting me off from his life- but no! I chose to take the revenge by just ignoring him like I was Kanishk. Maybe living with him affected me more than I thought. I shouldn't be forgetting that he is my sibling and we share the same bloodline.

Before my remorse drowned me into a self-destruction, I heard some quick footsteps approaching towards me. I could say it was me because the lane was completely emptied by then. I knew Delhi was pretty unsafe for women and standing in the empty lane, the fear of those footsteps made my blood into ice-cold rocks. Before I turned back to see that face, I felt two warm arms flung across my shoulders and softly hugged me in. The hug was familiar and gentle. There was no arousal, no appeal in it. Just two people's way of showing the care around. His jaw was on my right shoulder and his breaths were loud enough to be countable.

"I always knew you'd come back one day."- I said.

"How do you know it's me?"

He turned me to his face.

"How could I be wrong about you?"

"Why not? I ditched you. I left you on a wreck. I know it wasn't easy for you cause it wasn't easy for me either. And still…… after all these days?"

I smiled downing my face to the streets.

"Can you tell me a single way of forgetting your smell, your touch, anything that happened between us."- I took a break to engulf my sobs. I didn't want him to see me crying. Those words were tough. "How are you doing these days, Adith?"

"Won't you ask me why I left you the way I did?"

I gave a smile of negation.

"Oh, come on. Come here."

He pulled me towards his chest where my face used to rest all the time and once again, ignoring all the sulks and tears, I dissolved into him. The street was empty but very few people were actually passing by sometimes and I absolutely loved how they ignored our presence like the way Kanishk ignores me as his family.

But the thing I should've been concerned about a little earlier was the time. It was almost 8:30 at night and I was still on the streets in a place from where I had no clue how to reach home. My phone always stays at silent and now I saw the 4 missed calls from aunt and I called her back instantly. She seemed to get some relief hearing me and I told her to send a cab to the location I was in. I didn't know the streets, the place; the whole city was new to me, so getting Adith right there definitely made me feel safe.

"You wanna meet up tomorrow? There's a pub near this place. You can come here and I will take you there."

"Okay."- I still didn't know how to possibly say 'no' to him.

"Do you have the same number?"

"Yeah."

"See you tomorrow then."

I did neither ask for his number nor argue why he still kept mine! I just let it go, just the way I always do with things I have no control of. Choosing peace over everything else in life has become my character now. And I don't know how many things I am gonna lose for it.

He was there until the cab took me over and I got vanished from his sight.

I came home wrapped in all the primitive feelings and a pile of maddening flashbacks. Suddenly coming here felt so meaningful and worthwhile. Kanishk seemed like a very little thing to care about. He was like a hurdle to pass where the prize was Adith. Everything that was beautiful and true, was him. I forgot about everything that he did wrong or might have done in a different way that would've hurt less. But it was all just a healed-wound in a moment. I don't know what kind of power he possessed that made all my holdbacks gone in a jiffy. I forgot to be mad at him. I forgot to blink my eyes. I was just watching and wishing that those moments would stay alive for a little while.

THE MELTDOWN BEGINS

My aunt was always the sweetest person on earth. She became a widow when Kanishk was 2 months old. She never thought of remarriage and chose to stay alone with the memories and the huge properties my uncle left for her. Being childless never impacted her negatively. Even when Kanishk started living with her, it seemed like she could handle Kanishk better than my mom. She kind of understands us and we both ask for nothing more than it. So, living with her was more peaceful than living at home where thoughts are louder than words.

She came to my room at night to say that she wouldn't be home for a day, and somehow I had to manage to stay with Kanishk until she came back. Kanishk's behavior towards me was never unknown to anyone in my family. So, she told me to be a little adjustable that could avoid any trouble. But there was something else rounding up in my mind. I told her I had one more event the next day too, so I wouldn't be at home as an excuse for Kanishk to make a mess. It was a lie. I didn't have any event or anything alike, I just made a smooth way for me to go out and meet Adith. There were no trust issues between me and my family, especially in the matter of love life, which was practically non-existent to them, so I couldn't see a point if it looked like a lie.

My aunt told Kanishk to book a cab for me to the same place, and he didn't raise any query. Adith texted me in the morning that he would be right there and I had to reach there between 4-5 in the afternoon. He got a new number and I didn't know why he still kept mine. So, I went to the alley pretty early where we met last night. It felt like the young times when I used to wake up at 5, and get dressed till 6 to reach his place at 7 or 7:30ish. Adith never failed to encourage my enthusiasm towards our relationship and that was something always fed me thinking that he might be my ONE. But, there was a glitch in the matrix which I found out later.

When the cab left me a little backward to the alley, I saw Adith, already there, looking at his watch steadily. He knew I didn't like to pick up calls and frequent calls made me even less bothered. So, he just left a text that he was waiting. And there I found out he actually came 15 minutes earlier than the promised time. The whole year of staying alone and therapizing myself, left me with a lot of changes. One of them was not picking up calls unless it's really urgent or professional. The habit of hating calls gradually grew up in me so much that I started loving to disappear from my virtual life. Social media turned into an anxiety problem to me rather than a dreamy, fake world. Maybe I was the most boring person anybody could ever come across if they ever came across me by a zero probability.

"Hello there! So, you are late again!"- He smiled wrinkling his eyebrows as the sun was soft and about to set down.

"Yah, I never thought this city got so busy this time. It's nap-time in Kolkata."

"People here are always on toes."

"Where are we going today?"- And I saw him take me towards a car and open the door for me. A huge, expensive luxury car with big windows and a Karnataka number plate.

"Karnataka number?"

He looked a little quirky, "Somebody's noticing everything."

I was standing outside the car leaning on the closed window. He was inside, opening the door for me.

"If you don't wanna tell, it's fine. I am not that curious."

He came outside and stood in front of me hiding the sun. A 6ft 3 inch tall shadow guarded me over and I saw his face full of complaints.

"Why don't you ever ask me anything? Why are you always so unbothered? Why couldn't you just slap me directly when we met yesterday? I was a fucking jerk. I left you like you never happened. I left the most perfect life anyone could ever wish for. If I were you, I would've hated every bit of the existence of someone like me. Why Kenny? Why? Why don't you hate me? Why didn't you just pull my collar and crush the complaints on my face! Maybe this is the reason I still feel guilty every day, which is…leave it."

I didn't actually know what to say. The forceful things are always useless to me and it has become a habit of mine to let people go away with their secrets. So, if someone avoids my question, I never ask them back. I thought Adith never cared enough to notice these little things, now I knew these things actually made up something big in him. He was never loud to me except that day, so I was a bit scared if he started asking why I reached his house to look for any trace of him which I wasn't very proud of doing, only if he knew it, which was barely possible until Mr. Sen himself told him.

"Don't you use that tone with me! You are the one who should be ashamed of your doings. So, don't yell at me, now. I've nothing to do with that."

He was standing at a distance, now he came closer and held my face towards his, with both of his palms. My face was filled with fear and disgust.

"I am sorry, I am so sorry. Get in the car. We will talk on the way."

I got in the car. He started driving silently. After some time he broke the silence.

"What's the matter with you? There's nothing you can ask or complain about me? You forgive me all the way."

"There's nothing to forgive and who the hell am I to forgive you? That's a huge responsibility."

"Is it me or you are sounding like an 80-year- old?"

I smiled.

"Adith, it's not you. It's my destiny. I have been destined to live with the fact that I have to say goodbye to all the faces I love. I was never that much loved to demand a possession or an answer, and I am okay with that. You are no new to me. My own brother hates me to the bones, what can I expect from you? It's okay, darling. I love you and you know that. And you not necessarily have to love me back."

For some moments, he was clueless. Probably he didn't see that coming. So, he took a long pause before saying, "You still love me?"

I nodded with a smile. Hence, all the way to the streets, we didn't speak a word. After an hour, he parked the car in front of a five-star hotel and their driver took the car over from there.

"Adith, why are you spending so much on a stay? This hotel is awfully expensive."

"We met after a year. Trust me, it's worth it."

"No, it's not. I never wanted you to spend this much on me. You have a future. The car, this hotel - have these become your lifestyle now? How much are you making in a month? I must say I am impressed but I ain't pleased."

"Come with me, Mommy."

We checked in and it seemed like he did the booking yesterday. Therefore we went to our suite and the whole ambiance was kind of magical. He made me a coffee and sat in front of me with some cookies and croissants.

"You aren't happy, do you?"- He asked. "It's on your face. I think you finally got a question for me."

"You got a job?"

"Yeah! In that law firm. I got promoted a few months ago and all these are for that."

"How much are you earning? The car itself is worth 50 to 60 lakhs. I don't think you have already earned this in a year. And these luxuries are add-ons. How? What are you doing these days?"

"I got my grandfather's property. So, thought kinda buying what I love. The car is 85 lakhs though. More coffee?"

My question didn't make him uncomfortable, so my suspicions stopped right there. I knew his father was rich but I knew almost nothing about his family. Neither he talked about it nor did I ask him, ever. But the sudden changes in his lifestyle made him a little too different. He seemed a little prouder which I hate so intensely in a human being. Pride destroys people by making them blind about the right things in the surroundings. Proud people can't admit the facts that hurt and that's where the collision begins. And the worst example in my family is my *loving* brother who thinks the whole world is wrong except he, himself.

He came with a tray of another round of coffee and water. The cookies and croissants were drying up in the air. As the photo shoots were going on, I stopped touching sweets unless it was an unavoidable moment.

"Kenny, speak up. What's bothering you or in a better way, what's not bothering you? Why have you become such a dead soul? Is it me? Or anything else happened?"

"No, it wasn't you. Maybe this is the actual me. This is more of my reality. I love being silent. It helps to accept things quickly. You are changed too. Good. Good for you?"

"Can we lean on the couch? Like the way I used to hold you and you used to sleep on my chest?"

"Yah."- The spark of the moment and his proposal hit me up like a dream. I never thought of getting the chance to hold him again. It was more than a dream- a magic maybe.

I slept over him facing the huge window of the suit from where a little piece of the city was visible temptingly. His one hand was flung around my waist and the other one was crossing fingers with mine. His lips were on my neck, kisses and breathes were prominently frequent like a train whistle. I was thinking of a point to start when I heard him saying, "The old feelings aren't dead. You are still my one. You…"

"The one you love to play with, not to love hard."- I interrupted.

"I know what I did was wrong, but there are consequences. It was the only option for me and I hope someday I will tell you every little thing about it."

"It's alright."

"Aren't you angry? If it was somebody else, I would be dead by now."

"Nope. You know me, right? I wasn't angry; I was hurt which is really a usual emotion in my life since long. I am used to it."

"Were you surprised seeing me there? I thought I had lost you for life."

"Yah, a little bit."

"Why not a lot?"

"I always knew you would come back. You had to."

He kissed my neck and it was like pressing the on-side of the switch of my darkness. For that moment, the darkness wasn't sexual. I was rather expecting him to stay quiet and rub his nose against my neck until I finish piling up the questions that was rounding in my head over and over. The hardest part was to let it go when it mattered the most. I even said earlier that a writer can never unsee things. And that's where the problem starts. The upper layer of not-giving-a-fuck is standing over all the layers of overwhelming I-care-a-lot and I can't get a single thing over my head as it stays unanswered. I just want to be so comfortable with the opposite person that if he ever ignores my word, I would never come back to it, to make him uncomfortable.

"You know, Kenny, I have planned a lot of things to do with you even on those days we weren't together. There wasn't anyone else either. There can't be anyone else. All the night I stayed awake, I remembered the starry night we enjoyed together."

"Why didn't you call me then?"

"It's hard to explain. You wanna know what I planned for us to do?"

"You wanna tell?"

"Come on, Kenny. At least, be real for once. I know you are excited too. Stop being so mature for one day."

"If I were mature enough I would have probably moved on and dreamt my life with someone who would stay, rather than whining over you again and again."

"I know you are angry and that's very valid. But Kenny, you've loved someone who isn't like a normal lover. Maybe I can't elaborate my reason, but trust me, every time I hurt you, I got hurt a thousand times more. I…."

"Stop right there. Tell me about the plan."

"Yah. First have a booze, only for you and me, and a trip later on,."

"Nice."

"Just nice?"

"Yah, it's nice. You know, I don't drink."

"One day, please. You and I. Why not today? I will drive you home. One drink."

"Okay. Order some in."

"That's my girl."- He seemed excited and I was getting thrilled too. It was going to be my first drink in life where the add-on was him.

He ordered some scotch, wine bottles, and some soft drinks with soda. The bottle names were unknown to me, so I couldn't guess the price. But the outlook of it was suggesting a higher value. He got money and he had a big heart to spend it.

He first fixed two glasses on the table and started pouring from the bottle. I didn't know the limit I could take in one sip, nor did he suggest to me any. So, I took my first sip and it tasted like sour, expired tonics. But I didn't throw it out, I somehow engulfed it. I saw him enjoying every sip very gently, and I just tried to imitate him.

After a few drinks, I started to feel the trip. I don't know if it's called a trip, but it was a real trip, clearly a trip to the fantasy world. My body gradually started losing control, so did my tongue. I wanted to speak out everything, but I controlled not to. But some emotions were obvious. Those just needed a thrust to come out.

"How are you feeling?"- I saw him smirking at me, holding one glass in one hand and my hand in the other.

"Light. Really, really light."- Even I sounded like a hippie to myself too.

"Come to me. You okay?"- He pulled my head on his shoulder and it felt like all the weight fell over him.

I didn't stop drinking though and after some time, the outcome wasn't very sober.

One cycle of three drinks- "I am okay. Adith, you know, you are the most handsome and appealing boy in the world. But, you know what! You are an asshole. You fucking left me. You left me in the moment I started weaving all my dreams with you. I hate how much I love you, even after all these days. And I am afraid that I can't love someone this much ever again, not even my own self. You are my every night's desire from the day I saw you. I sleep every night with disappointment and wake up consoling myself that you would never be mine. I hated everything about my life before you came into it and now I hate it even more. Why the fuck you left me when I was never the reason? I have loved you with the very bottom of my heart, and look what you've done to me. I am now an unsocial, eccentric, and a depressed creep. I am scared of meeting people, talking to them. I hate everyone for everything they haven't even done and it's true."

I sat down, poured myself one more glass, then one more and started talking trash again.

"You know, my life is on a wreck. I am gonna get graduated next year and I don't have any fucking idea what I am gonna do next. Being a writer won't pay me any, so I will probably be a hobo, or an eligible face on matrimony or an unemployed burden on my dad. My brother is probably planning to get me married and banish me from the house. You know, he is even a bigger jerk than you. He hated me all his life just because I was born to his parents. You know, if I die today, he will be the happiest person on earth. Even I think, he secretly prays to god every day to remove me from his life anyway. After all these freaking years, I came here with a hope that maybe we can be a normal sibling now. But, he's still a jerk and I am still a moron to love him just because we have the same blood."- At this point, I started laughing. Sometimes lower, sometimes at a higher pitch, and kept on blabbering while sipping the refills.

"You know my brother Kanishk, right? If he clears UPSC this time, he's gonna be an IAS or IPS whatever. Means, my whole clan will worship him and he will be more miserable. Everyone will be his puppet and someday he will leave me in no man's land. I strongly believe it. For the worst, he can kill me and make it look like an accident. I don't actually know the intensity of his hatred towards me, but it's kinda deep."- I took one more drink.

"I hope he fails. Not only in this exam, in every upcoming exam and hurdles in his life. So that he can understand what kind of pain I go through every day by being a failure to everything. I want him to be dependent on me, so that I can treat him well with every single fucking way he couldn't, and he realizes that how cruel he was to me for no good reason. Nikhil! You know my best friend Nikhil, don't you? A part of me kinda hates him too. You wanna know why? Because I know he will leave me again if he gets a girlfriend or a better friend than me. See, how easily replaceable I am in anyone's life. I am invisible in this world. No one cares. No one ever cared. No one ever grabbed my hand and begged me to stay. I used to believe you until you went away, ghosting yourself. I don't know where the fuck I went wrong that my brother hates me this much, my boyfriend doesn't want to stay with me, my best friend treats me as a backup and my parents have no hopes on me. I am just a rolling stone on earth with a heartbeat. You know how it feels to live a life like this, every single day? Nobody ever tried to talk to me. I want to talk about my problems, my mental health, my anxiety. I want to ask Kanishk why he can't accept me like all other good brothers! I want to slap you until I am feeling I am done taking the revenge of the tears you caused me every night. I want to tell Nikhil that I know he's trying to get rid of me or maybe something else. I want to ask my parents why they forgot to teach their son a little bit of humanity. When he was cruel to me from the very first day, and most effectively, why didn't they protest? But I can't. I hate talking to people. I hate seeing anyone's face. I hate looking at you. I know I am gonna fall again and you will leave me here deserted. I just wanted simple days of loving you, waking up in the same bed, making you laugh and all. But YOU, you sick fuck, I know, you would never let that happen. Why did you never love me, Adith? I know I am not as pretty as you desire someone to be, or probably I am not the one to call you every 30 minutes like the stereotypical girlfriend, but I dare you to find someone who would love you as much as I do. I bet you end up empty-hearted."

I lost my balance and fell over the other side of the couch. In my blurry vision, I saw him sitting there like a sculpture. His glass was on the table and both of his hands were fisted together under his jaw, drowned in deep thinking.

"Am I blabbering a lot? Oh no!"-There was a gagging silence. He didn't even move. I wasn't in sense what to say further, so I played safe.

"Adith, I wanna go home."

"Sure."- He didn't say anything else.

He drove me all the way from the hotel to home and was frequently placing my head to the headrest as I was losing my balance and falling on the other side. While dropping me off, he told me to go to my room as quietly as possible and not to talk to anyone in between. He even took me to the door and rang the bell as it was hard for me to press it.

After Adith went away, Kanishk opened the door. First he scrutinized me from top to bottom, and said, "It's almost 10. What the fuck were you doing out there this late? You said you would be home at 8:30 max like yesterday."

My sober self would've stayed silent and ignored him like a wuss, but till then, my trip went on to another level. So, I responded by blowing a raspberry down, "Oh please! Like you care!"

He was stunned. He never expected a rude response from my side as I never did that before. It took him a few minutes to process that I actually said it.

"What did you say? What's the tone with that?"- He was going red in anger.

"You heard, what I fucking say."

"Kenny, are you drunk?"- Then he realized I was actually drunk. "You are fucking drunk. This is what you came here for. Who was there with you? Answer me, now?"

"Yeah, I am drunk. Tomorrow morning I will be sober and you will still be a jerk. And this is not what I came here for. This is my first time drinking, and I'm kinda loving it. Stop asking me questions like you care a lot. I know you just want these answers to call dad and portray me as a miserable character to him. I hope you never existed in my life, like the way you wish me dead. I would never want my enemy to have a brother like you. You are the worst. You made me hate my life, myself, my existence, and look at me now; I am depressed, stupid and suicidal. I hate myself that I still love you after all the things you have done to me and will gonna do in future. You are a worm of hell. What you think, I don't know you are still a creep as before! You left me on a wreck when I needed you the most. You never let your friends know that you have a sibling. You remember, in 3rd standard, you left me covered with blood after I fell over and cut my knees and hands. Kanishk, I was 7, I was expecting you to come and take me home after aiding me. And what you did instead? You left early for home hiding in the trees so that nobody would ask to take me with you. That year, on Diwali, you left me on the streets at night, telling me you would come back with chocolate and you never came. You told mom I was the one who ran away! All these years of detachment never made you think about your cruelty towards me.

You never ever cared to call me on my birthday. It's probably the worst day of your life. Isn't it? Why Kanishk? Why are you like this? How can you never wonder why I never complained about you to dad about the things you did to me? You know, we still have the same blood. We were in the same womb. And it's my responsibility to love you, doesn't matter whatever you do. Nana taught me to love my family first even when I got the worst one. You were ashamed of me every single day for not being a topper jerk like you, where I was telling my friends how brilliant my brother is and how my whole family is so so proud of you. You are the worst brother, but I never hated you the way you hate me. And I know your point very clearly. I should've never been born. But can you tell me how it was under my control? I never came to your life willingly. Trust me, if I had a choice, I would choose to be homeless and sleep under the bare sky rather than sharing a roof with you. I hate to see your face. When I look at you, I see a monster trying to eat me alive. I never saw love, empathy, affection in those eyes. You are worse than evil and I wish one day you will become human enough to understand that. You can tell everyone about tonight and I will still not care. You know why? Because I accept you as an accident in my life that I have to live with. I am not an inhuman like you. I know how to love and I would never ever be like you even if you become the most successful person on earth. I would rather choose to be human than being rich and complimented. I wish you get to read my suicide note one day I wrote for you all, and think why you did what you did. For now, you are dead to me. Get out of my way."

I didn't know how much I drank, but all of a sudden it felt relented. I was unrestrained, a freeflow with little boundaries. It was a magic.

I went to my room, and I saw him sitting on the sofa in the middle of the drawing room. His face was no longer red, rather it was pale with his jawline clenched hard. He was shocked like nobody had ever jabbed him with the pieces of ugly truth. I was surprised too, seeing him not giving a comeback. He was never this quiet. Maybe this was the day he was afraid of witnessing and I made his nightmare come true.

I slammed my door and let the air hang in between us. He was still sitting there like he got glued to the seat and I didn't think he was gonna get over it easily. That was my day. That night, I was the law. I ruled over my boys. I was thankful I was drunk. My sober self would've never let me do that.

SEASON 'ME'

The next morning, I woke up with a headache. The dizziness lasted longer than I thought. I unlocked my phone screen and saw 4 text messages from Adith. He wanted to know if I was okay and apologized for bringing the idea of drinking to the table of losing control. I kinda enjoyed it though, but the real fear was waiting for me downstairs. Kanishk might have already told mom how scary I was last night and she probably started scolding dad for permitting me to come here. But strangely, I didn't see any messages or call from home. It was 9:30 in the morning and nobody actually interrogated me about last night. Aunt was probably at home as she was supposed to come in the early morning and still there was nothing. It felt fishy so, I called mom to know if they had already decided to disown me or they were still giving it a thought.

She picked up my call at third ring.

"Hey mom."

"Kenny, you are up! I called your aunt an hour ago and she said you are sleeping. How was your fashion-thing yesterday?"

I took a little time to process if it was a pun before she actually started to yell or there was something else.

"Good. How was your day, Ma?"

"As usual. You aren't home. It doesn't feel right. The house is like so big and hollow and I have no one to argue over food."

I laughed, but I couldn't understand why she wasn't mentioning anything about last night.

"Yah, anything else?"

"Nothing. You have your breakfast?"

"No, I just woke up. Gonna go down in a while."

"Okay, you go, have your meal. I have to go to the groceries."

"Sure. There's nothing more you wanna ask?"

"What should I ask? You already told me everything."

"How's dad?"

"He's good. I know you are missing home. But it's too late for breakfast. You should hang up and eat first. Bye, honey, love you."

What! Mom doesn't know anything! How's that possible. Kanishk leaves this golden opportunity to tear me down. Is it real?

I went downstairs and aunt called me to sit for breakfast. She didn't say anything either. She didn't have any clue where and how I was last night. She made some delicious food to light up the morning. When I asked about Kanishk, she said he had eaten already and he was in his room, studying.

I finished off my breakfast and knocked at his door cause somehow I thought I owed him an apology. At least, for keeping his mouth shut.

He opened the door and I slipped into his couch, keeping the door closed not locked.

"I am sorry about last night. The far I realized you didn't tell anyone and for which I am pretty grateful."

He didn't say a word. He just looked at me like he could see through my mind. His eyes were fixed into my face, observing and absorbing every single emotion coming out with my words.

"Kanishk, I am really sorry. I met a friend over there. We had some food, and she offered me some drinks which I never had before and after a few, I got drunk. I am sorry if my words hurt you. I wasn't in proper sense."

These were all lies. I might not be in my proper sense, but I wasn't sorry for whatever I said. But to be safe to him, I had to tell this.

"If you are done, go to your room."- He looked down to his books and told me to get out indirectly.

I was getting out, but I turned back readily to ask him something more.

"Kanishk, why didn't you tell anyone about last night?"

He looked up and said what I never expected him to say.

"Kenny, I don't show emotions that doesn't mean I don't have any. I don't want any more talking about this. Go to your room."

For some moments, I thought I was in a Van Gogh painted blue sky world; trying to find every plausible reason about what he actually meant, and if he meant what I was thinking, and even for more - why he meant it.

All of a sudden, it felt different, like he was trying to come at ease. The words from the last night scenes tagged a bow in his soul. He couldn't get rid of it and the far I knew him, he would never gonna forget the night.

Coming upstairs, I texted back Adith that everything was okay and he didn't need to be ashamed about the outburst I had after his alcohol session. I wanted to say things I couldn't say. So, sometimes we should let the drinks tear open the real us.

In between, Adith called and asked if I would be interested to head out somewhere. So, when I said yes, he came in front of my aunt's house to take me in. Aunt was cool with me hanging out with friends, and she was pretty happy telling my mom that I made friends there. Kanishk and I both are dumb in making friends. We are terribly unsocial and shy when it comes to initiation, so having good friends isn't less than a wondrous thing to our parents.

We went to a nearby restaurant where we had some amazing pasta and shakes. Adith was talking about some chemical compound he found out online while I was trying to remember what exactly I said to Kanishk that brought something up in his peculiar mind for me.

"You aren't listening to me at all. Are you?"- Adith saw I was being blunt.

"Not at all. What are you blabbering about?"

"Something you don't seem interested in. What's on your mind?"

"Nothing serious. Go on. I will listen."

"Nope, Kenny, cut the crap. What's going on in your head?"

"You know, the way I behaved with you last night, I did the same with Kanishk. And the surprising thing is, he didn't complain about it to anyone. Mom, dad, aunt - none. Nobody knows a word; else I would be home by now. You kinda know how our relationship is. So, I was thinking what exactly I said to him that actually restrained him from complaining about me."

"You don't remember anything?"

"I remember calling him a jerk. Rest isn't very clear."

"Leave it. I do have a great plan, but I don't know if you are going to agree with that or not."

"I am all ears."

"I am staying in Bangalore currently. So, I was thinking if you want to come over. We can spend some days there together."

"Are you crazy? My parents will never let me go."

"Your parents aren't here. Who will let them know?"

"Kanishk. And of course, he won't let me go. It's not happening."

"Can I talk to Kanishk?"

"Don't be insane. No."

"Why not? He's your brother? How bad can he be?"

"No means no, Adith. I am not going."

"For once. Let me try. Please. Just a request. Give me his number."

I kept quiet.

"Kenny, don't you wanna go?"- He asked again.

"I don't have his number."

"What! Why? He's your cousin brother or own brother?"

"My own brother, unfortunately."

"What's the matter between you two? Feud or what?"

"I don't know. I just know that I can't go."

"Can I have your aunt's number?"

"No."

"What? You don't have her number either?"

"I do have, but I can't give it to you. I am sorry."

"Kenny, why are you making me talk this much? Just one call."

I never won against that voice, to be better if called a submissive witchcraft.

I handed it over, copying from my phonebook and when it rang, he distanced himself to be completely inaudible to me. I saw him dialing one more number and called someone one more time, but the smile on his face didn't faint at all. The far I could read his face - he was listening more than putting inputs and the whole conversation was peaceful enough to keep the satisfaction in his eyes.

He came after a 15 minutes talk while I finished my pasta and the whole truffle. A smile in his eyes was lingering and vibrating through his heart. I got the hint something actually happened that might not be very plausible to me at all.

"Hey, guess who's got a permission to fly with me?"

I raised my eyebrows.

"Stop acting like you can't imagine anything. You are going to my place. Probably not in the same flight, but who cares?"

"And who gave the permission?"

"Your brother. He's really good. I don't know why you always have problems with him!"

"Wait a minute! Kanishk told you that I can go with you? "

"Yup"

"He spelled that? Did you hear it right?"

"Absolutely. He even said he's gonna book your ticket. He doesn't want me to pay for you."

"I don't know what is going inside his head, but I can sense this isn't good. He is probably cooking something to put me into trouble. And you know what you did? You put the key in his hand. He's probably gonna tell dad that I came here to do stuff with you. What you did, Adith! He's gonna ruin me forever."

"I think you are overthinking. Kenny, there's nothing to worry about."

"Really? You talk to him one day and you fall into his trap. I know this bastard from the day I was born and that was the day he started hating me. I have to go home. RIGHT NOW. You have already done the damage, just do me a favor; drop me home as soon as you can."

I saw the smile fading away from his two brightening eyes, wavering some questions in his heart, remained unanswered. He just nodded a little and took me to the car.

I was worried, angry and boiling up with anxiety. Nobody knows what was going inside my brother's evil brain which could destroy my forever trustworthiness and the image I built in front of my family suppressing my anger and hatred to every situation I never fitted in. But there's still a trembling ray of hope at the very end of the tunnel, that he might be a little less cruel or forgetful as the way he acted this morning, but the path was full of uncertainty. He had been inhuman to me for my whole life and changing him by my outrage wasn't plausible enough to put a trust on.

Adith was silently driving me home and the face of guilt was sabotaging his whole presence with huffs which were overwhelming through the silence in the car. Even in the storm of silence, I couldn't help but falling for him like the way I did on the very first day we met. With the freaky wind coming from his side of the window, a tuft of his hair was flipping around his forehead. His face was a dream; crafted with some trimmed beard and a splash of God's favorite potion. I couldn't stop wondering how many days and hours I had craved for this face to kiss; this hair to cross fingers in; these lips to touch with mine, and now when he was with me, I was doing exactly the opposite of what I was supposed to. But he had the power to drive me crazy even when I was at my worst. So, even though I was angry with him for messing things up inside my deep, dark brotherly-issues, I was still craving to bite his lips, and stretched it as deep as it could go towards my tongue right that moment. I can never explain the moment of having him back with the nights, I only shredded tears and curses to myself to my own damn bad luck of being born like such an unwanted and rejected burden on earth. He was the only shine in my life to where I could breathe a chestful of happiness. Your parents can't fulfill all your desires and that's why your life needs a piece of cake to satisfy your taste buds; just like a lover- to quench your lust, to complete your entity, to be your poem of life which nobody has ever endured to become one. As Nikhil had changed by the age and his environmental constraints, Adith was both my best friend and lover - a lover I gained after so many nights of waiting, which was obviously worth every pain. I don't know why people these days are so afraid of commitments and staying with someone worth staying, while chasing loose ends at the cost of losing a real connection.

Adith and I were appropriate. And if you ask me how I know he's the one - I can prepare a PPT on it. He made me a writer, he gave me the wings to fly, tearing up my insecurities, he made me strong enough and mostly he taught me how to hate myself less. But I was dumb enough to realize all that, after it was too late.

He dropped me at a distance of my doorstep and while slamming the door, I just looked at him holding grudges for something he never realized doing. His face had a guilt-trip with a suppressed smirk under his lips, which held the tail of my weakness even after the anger. If I would've stayed a little longer, he would probably get a chance to say 'bye', but I didn't stop. I rushed to my room, passing the dining where my aunt was watching the same bullshit serial that my mom watches with a bowl of popcorn.

"Honey, you are early. Take your popcorn. It's on the kitchen table."- She saw me rushing through the stairs.

"Thanks, I am not hungry."

But I came back after going up a few stairs, and asked, "Kanishk had his?"

"No! And surprisingly, he said the same thing. You two kids are one. Don't know what's the matter with you two."

She didn't care enough to look at me while talking, so she failed to notice the unedged fear in my face of being accused of something I hadn't done. I went to my room, washed myself off and started waiting for my aunt to go to her room so I could have an empty dining room to pass by. I didn't want my aunt to see me going to my brother's room as it could raise a lot of questions which I wasn't proud of answering. This is where I couldn't corporate myself with a more normal behavior. This is where we lost the relation of blood.

In between, I received a text from an unknown number containing an air ticket to Bangalore. On checking the display picture, I found my brother's face on it. He clearly sent me a ticket to fly there which also meant he was allowing me to go, and for what reason God knows. Everything was more than fishy out there, and the more I started thinking, the deeper I felt falling, where there was nothing but more and more confusion. So, after an hour, I got the chance to sneak into Kanishk's room, I knocked twice and entered without waiting for his approval.

"Nobody ever taught you the meaningfulness of knocks?"- His eyes were facing the tough pages of his textbooks where I was looking for a possible interaction to clear things out.

"I want to talk."

"Well, I don't. So, get out."

"Kanishk, how long you think you will be able to ignore me?"

"What you want?"

"Why are you doing this? Have you already told mom? Therefore, you are allowing me to go! Why? What exactly is going on your head."

"I send you the ticket, what else will gonna happen there?"

"Why are you even allowing me to go? You don't even know who I am going with."

"Isn't it Adith? I have sources and I know your run."

"How do you know him?"- My voice got stuck.

He looked at me lifting his face up with those cold, restless eyes as unbothered as the rain in summer. His vision was straight, rigid and killing me all the way through.

"Kanishk, in my whole life, you have done every possible thing to put me in trouble. You hated me from the moment I was born, blamed me for all those things which were never on me. Still, I tolerated you, and never raised my voice as you are older and I am supposed to respect you. But if you try to cause him any harm, I will slit your throat into pieces and I swear to God, I am never gonna regret that."

"You love that guy like nuts, ain't it, Kenny?"- His eyes were still glued on my face.

I kept quiet.

"I will tell mom, I am sending you out there for my work. I hope you will not do anything that will put both of us in trouble."

For the very first time in my life, I felt valued, a little bit wanted and responsible. I don't know which potion was actually working on him, but that was the day he first behaved like a brother, a real older brother. All these years of anger, hatred and complaints melted down to a point zero. At that very moment, all I wanted was to rush towards him and hug him on my strongest hold until he felt the warmth of my gratefulness. I tried to decide for a few moments if I should do it or it would make me look more desperate, and I let my judgments win the race. This is the problem of hitting puberty - you forget to express your emotions, you dry up your tears silently, you therapize yourself alone, and moreover you heal to be an inhuman. Even as a child, I never hugged my brother. He was never around and even if he did, he hated to make a minimal colloquial conversation with me. So, there was no way to build a relationship where things were only half way up. But all of it suddenly started making sense. God has imposed women with immense power of forgiveness and till this day I am paying for it with all the ways that went right or the others that left me.

Coming back to my room, I packed some of my things that I thought were necessary, and told aunt that Kanishk was sending me to Bangalore to collect some of his papers. My parents didn't ask a word as my brother was clear about his lies and the two of them got some hope that it might be a turning point in our sibling rivalry which it clearly was. Kanishk didn't seem bothered by the time I was leaving but he came downstairs to exchange a Goodbye smile. It was a hell of a trip. Going away from my family to spend a week with someone I was dying to get along with and fusing moments together, was often raising questions in my mind, "What after love? What connects and keeps the sustainability and what I want now?"- And clearly there were no answers.

HOW HUMAN ARE YOU, KANISHK?

It happened the day after I came back to Kolkata. Clearly, I was done with the shoots on which I slowly started losing interest but Kanishk and I were on talking terms and my connection with Adith was never stronger before. Everything was at its perfection, but this happiness was never mine. The day I came back to Kolkata, the day I started losing connection with Adith, and the loose ends were not from my side. He just stopped being like before and my enormous long texts started finding his one-word answer. And after some days, it also stopped. The more I texted, the more supplementary blue ticks I got, and my anxiety level turned into a sky-rocket. I tried to call and he let it ring without responses.

Life has taught me enough lessons to be okay with being ignored, and not needed. But even after a million lessons, my heart refuses to stop dreaming. My sleepless nights were back on which I used to drown into self-doubts, questions, worries, tears and memories. Not in any universe, I found a way of why he left me in the seenzone and refused to continue the magical connection we had before. The days in Bangalore in his apartment started feeling like a daydream disguised in vanity and lies. Every day I woke up beside him, I thanked God for making me do so. But definitely there were some cracks in my prayer, else I would have been getting a good night's sleep by then. One moment he was beside me slurping his tea bathed in morning sun, and the next moment he was gone. I could see his social existence; I was seeing him being online but none of those couldn't manage enough time to revert back to me. Those moments made me realize that I wasn't healed at all. I wasn't that strong I thought I would've become and I was still at the scratch of handling ghosting. Every time I saw him seeing my texts and ignoring them like they never mattered, splitted my world into pieces and didn't matter how many self-love quotes I read, I ended up hating myself for not being worth staying with. He ghosted himself before, and it took me a year to heal, and still I managed to find him down the line to be destroyed again. Men never understood the feminine urge to be heard, seen and loved, and by my terrible misfortune, all the masculine entities in my life are dangerously unbothered about how they have made me the queen of anxiety.

It was the end of March. The weather was getting me out of my winter clothes and the approaching summer was palpable after a cardio session. Adith was gone for months now, and all the connection that left with him was dying in his seenzone. The last four months of my college life was getting even more intolerant. Every day I walked through the streets, a splash of old, junk memories fell upon my face and took me to the days I spent with reality and happiness. I strained myself to the last drop to make him happy where he was bulging his masculinity to pleat me in a place called "nostalgia ''. I kept waiting for him to be a human, when he was busy contributing to the séance he owned, by choking my soul and watching it die painfully. Even after all these days of cruelty, am I free from his noose of lies? Probably not; probably never.

Afternoons are mostly meaningless as each activity seems distracting enough to get a good sleep. Most of the days when I am home, I can't keep my eyes open after my mom's heavy lunch.

So, I was making a comfortable pillow arrangement to get a tight sleep until I heard a soft knock on the door.

"Come on in."- I thought it was the maid who probably forgot something in my room. Generally, people don't like coming here and that ignorance makes me so grateful to their choices. But that day, it wasn't the maid, not anyone who had possibilities to crash by. It was Kanishk who never even cared to stop by the balcony beside my room.

Kanishk was living with us after his Mains exam was over and he was pretty confident about the results. Mom made him come home, and till then he was at home making peace with my existence.

"You are free now? I need to talk."

"Am I in trouble?"- My usual instinct came out instantly.

"Oh God, no. It's different."

"Come inside."

He came and sat on the corner of my bed.

"How you doing?"

"Come to the point, what you want?"

"I came here to ask how you doing?"- It was definitely a bummer from his side.

"Fine."

"Do you miss him? Adith! He texted you back?"- In between, I told Kanishk that Adith had stopped reverting me back, so he kind of knew I was going through a rough patch.

"No. He left."

"I hope you are doing okay."

"Yah, what option do I have? How are you doing?"

In the first few seconds, he kept staring at my face without blinking, from where I could easily pretend the kind of typhoon hailing inside and destroying him every second until he got an outburst. Therefore, he did something that even the whole universe would've refused to believe if not seen in naked eyes. I wondered why the sky didn't fall apart, why the land didn't crack into parts, but it happened when it happened. My brother hugged me. It wasn't even a hug; it was a complaint wrapped in a heartbreak and mostly a moment to slow down. He held me for some minutes where I spent the first ones to find a way to process it. After I got a little bit used to it, I placed my hand on his head and eventually brought it down to pat on his back. He was sniffling, and I finally realized something bad happened.

"I am here to listen whenever you are ready to talk."-I slowly whispered in his ears as it was very close to my mouth.

"I couldn't make it, Kenny. I am a failure. It's 3 years in a row."

It took me more than usual attempts to process that it was his result day. He cleared the prelims but again he got stuck in Mains, and it was not his fault to be upset after working so hard.

"You remember Vijay, who used to take notes from me, even he cleared it. All my batchmates cleared it and I failed again."

I held him even tighter. I felt he needed it the most.

"I let everybody down. I wasted dad's money, mom's hopes on me. I am unemployed, a living burden in this family. I looked into the mirror and all I see is a loser, a failure, a junk in a clutter. What should I do, Kenny? I am scared to die so early. I can't suicide, but trust me I don't have any will, any purpose to be alive anymore."- His sniffles got clearer and louder.

"If you say that one more time, I am gonna throw you away from my room. Even if the world is ending today, you can know one thing for sure, I love you, and you matter to me. Your life, your breath, your existence matters to me. So, don't you dare to leave me."

He unfolded himself, "After all these things I have done to you?"- He paused and said again, "Why?"

"You had your reasons, I have mine. You are my own brother. My blood vessels won't let me unlove you."

"Mom used to say that you possess the bigger heart, but I never knew you would be this. If I were you, I would've been hating a brother like me for the rest of my life!"

"Yeah, so, it's clear you are definitely not me. Kanishk, I don't know why you hate me this much, but I always prayed for your success. I want you to have everything you want in life. I never let my prayers go against you, and of course I have forgiven you for everything. Can I ask why you hate me so much, when I nevertheless ever caused a little scratch on you."

His sniffles were at ease, but the storm inside was still growing furious. But somehow, at that moment, I was his only refuge, a trusted ear where his failure wouldn't be criticized -"I was never good at sharing. I had all the love of mom, dad, granny, everybody - until you came. I used to see them getting changed and how their attention got shifted from me to you. You made me share my room, my parents, my foods, the love, and the attention I used to get. I hated it so much that I made you the culprit for all of it. I never wanted this but this silliness grew with me and even after being an adult, I never ever tried to mend the turmoil I created for you. I am sorry, Kenny. I am probably not the brother you deserve. And trust me, I hate myself for that too."

"I already have forgiven you for that. But I don't think I was planned to be in your life. That wasn't in my hand. And you kept harming me till we were apart. You left me in the roads alone, in the empty school, in everywhere I needed you. We are grown-ups now. We should've talked about this earlier."

"I know, and I feel terrible about it. I was trying to get rid of you, and I was so stupid to think that it would work someday. I don't know from where this darkness is actually from, but every time you were with me, I wish you never existed."- He slowed down the last line.

"The things you did to me, I could've probably died. I was a kid, Kanishk. I didn't have the power to realize why that was happening."- My voice went up a bit.

"Hey, stop making me feel miserable. I know what I did and I can never forgive myself for that, not in this life. I know I was the worst brother, and this is the way God is punishing me back."- He stopped and pushed down to the bed lowering his eyes.

"I have forgiven you, and I don't think you want me dead anymore. Do you?" - I smiled.

"Shut up! I told you I feel horrible for that."

"So, what are you gonna do next? Give it another shot?"

"I don't know. I don't want to. I am hating myself, my studies, this unemployment of mine. I don't know what's next. What do you want me to do?"

"I want you to give it another shot. And I know this time, you are gonna make it. Analyze your mistakes, not take guilt from it."

"What if I fail this year too?"

"Then you will go back looking for a job, or I will ask you to find a passion to pursue. And whatever happens, you will still gonna be my brother and I will still love you. This isn't the end. This is the beginning of the voyage."

He hugged me again; and this time it was firmer than the previous one.

"I am sorry, Kenny. I am sorry for all the bad days I caused you. You are probably the best gift God has ever planned for me, and I tried to throw it away. Please forgive me, sister. I promise I will try to be the brother you deserve, even though I can't fix the damage I already have done to you. If you won't forgive me, I bet this is the premiere of my upcoming bad days. Karma exists, Kenny. What I did to you was a federal crime. Nothing can release me from my sins."

Yes, I heard it right. He addressed me as his sister, for the very first time in my life and his as well. He said 'Sorry'. He realized he did something wrong. It wasn't a win. It was more than a win for me. Getting my brother back, seeing him being a man with humanity and emotion! It was rare. It wasn't the first failure for him, but through this third time, he realized life isn't always dreamy. Even the most brilliant mind fails, goes through trouble, hatred, self-doubts and life is all about accepting it with open arms. Maybe for the first time as an adult, he felt the way I have been feeling my whole life. I wasn't proud of being happy for him, but I was happy to see him growing as a real man.

That summer never came when I was hoping to get Adith back again and cup his face with the palm of my cold hands. It had been long but I didn't let a single day pass by without thinking about him. Mostly the mornings were dangerously difficult. Every morning gave me the feeling of quitting the world without his touch in my head. I was so addicted to his smell, that almost every day, I used to smell the notebook he gave me. He wasn't gone. He was just not mine and accepting this was even more painful than looking for his existence.

He made my every morning more sufferable than it ever did. I stayed in bed for a few more minutes waiting for my tears to get soaked in the pillow covers. The thought of losing him, when I tried to be his reflex, was drumming hammers in my heart. I never wanted to control his life or asked for his attention 24x7. I just wanted him to stay; for me; for the universe; for the prayers, through thick and thin. To inhale him, manifest him and to worship him. I wasn't a difficult woman. I wanted to be his woman to bring all the good in him. Not all the relationships can be named or labelled. I wanted that something for us, which would be untouched by the poison of society, fear of mistrust, toxicity of unfaithful commitments, and scarcity of unhappy marriages. Maybe it was too much to ask that I finally lost him.

I woke up every morning, and cursed myself hatefully for being alive again without a life. But it was Dwight Schrute from The Office US who kept me moving on. All the time, I wanted to cry, I used to remember him and his quotes towards life,

"Will I get over it?

MMM, no. But life goes on."

I wanted to be as strong, as loyal as Dwight, but I lost myself towards his sacrifices. Moreover, I wasn't him and that's how he was livelier to me even as a TV character than to my fake blood-relatives.

But somebody said it right. Time heals everything, but time can't obliterate feelings, mostly the loving ones. I tried to engage myself to the most, tried to find someone else to focus on, tried to emerge myself into writing, but everything I did, every face I met, I was desperately looking for him everywhere. Even my disappointments stopped bothering me after some time. Nobody was him. Nobody could be him and that was the most painful part no consolation could ever heal.

I wanted to be that girl that he could miserably be in love with. I wanted to be his strength to brainwash him to be the most pure-hearted human being. I wanted to bathe in his affection when my whole world was falling apart. I wanted a universe only for him and I. I am possessive, I am not good at sharing, and in no universe, I could imagine him to be shared, spared and had been taken away from me. I was erratic and still he was the most certain decision of my life. His smiles were mine. His cold feet in winters, his first yawn in the morning, the smell of sweat melted with his perfume after a busy day, the scar under his skin, the heart hidden in a tough patch - all were mine, even when he didn't know. This is the magic of loving in silence - you can own something without a gullible effort of proving it to others. Silence means no fear of rejection, not hurting my own feelings, never proving the power of possession. The silence was mine, as well as his never-ending survival in me. And I was his from the very first day I met him. He owns me, every enduring cell of my existence - completely, impartially, unapologetically.

All my madness was relentlessly on him- to love him, to fix him, to adore him and to fulfil his voids. But in the time of being his woman, I forgot about the girl inside me. I was definitely a giver but sometimes I also craved for a love-back. He felt for me for some incomplete moments, and when they were over, he was over too. And in this commotion, I fell in love, I broke my heart, I healed, and I fell again, where he probably never felt a single thing the way I did.

"RUN"

From the day Kanishk officially realized the bonafide irony of being a brother, a year has passed. All our priorities have changed except my weakness for the man I met on a sunny day, in my city, unwillingly. From the moment I saw him, a part of me already knew that my life would never be the same again.

After ghosting himself for almost 6 months, one day a notification popped in my screen with his name. He texted me to come outside, as he was there, out of nowhere. And the strong feminine urge to hold myself onto in front of the world, hiding tears with silence, ignorance and sometimes with smiles, and breaking into pieces when he calls even after stabbing my heart to death while forgiving and forgetting all the anxiety, stress, suicidal nights he caused me - I met him again without even a second thought. I graved my self-respect, ego and all the other strong humanly emotions to see his face again. Every time he looked at me, I couldn't afford to look straight, but every time he looked away, I looked into him, to the deepest end, counted the love, lust, and the shores he built in those eyes. He possessed me with every stare. He saw me with every detail. He knew my birth marks, stretch marks, curves, accidents, freckles and every pleasuring spot of my body. He knew how to enroot his entity into me and make me hopelessly stuck with him even when the whole world was trying to break me out. With every inspection, I found my missing pieces in him and he was never in the mood of returning them.

In that one year, everything was changed. Kanishk moved on from his dream to become an IAS, which I supported effortlessly. I saw him breaking down, losing his spirit and doubting all the achievements he had done so far. The boy who never knew the fear of losing his confidence, I saw him landing at zero. That exam was getting toxic for him. Some nights, he used to come to my room silently, lay on my lap, and ask if I had any purpose for him to live the next morning. Though a part of my childhood was spent hating him and looking for reasons for his brutality towards me, I never wished him tears. His tears still wring my heart as it used to, and I suffer the same way seeing him fall into the ground. So, I did some research and fueled him with an MBA degree abroad. For both almighty's grace and his own hard work, he made it to the Stanford Graduate School of Business and moved to the United States for 2 years. So, this was the first time I was missing him, mostly at nights when we used to be raw and share every secret with each other. But I was happy, seeing him happy there and it was just a matter of time to see him again after his Master's. He used to call me sometimes and our parents were overwhelmed to see us fixing everything on our own. But for me, fixing would have been better if we were together. Since Nikhil and Adith were long gone, I built my world around Kanishk. I started noticing the similarities, the differences, the likings, the postures between us. He has my blood, and I have his strength. The first time I started feeling blessed about sharing a womb with him as soon as I discovered him being that fragile from inside wrapped in a strong shell. None other than him could understand my emotions that perfectly. And again, when things started getting right, he had to leave. But this time, I knew he was not leaving me emotionally and I was assured that I had his back every time I felt alone.

In between, when Adith came back, I made him meet Kanishk. Kanishk had his own judgments. Though Adith admired him from the very first day he spoke with him over phone, Kanishk never put restrictions on me when Adith and I used to go out. I knew I was digging my own grave allowing him to come back and leaving me in a nutshell again, but in the feud between my senses and feelings - my heart crossed the line devastatingly.

In this one year, I met a lot of new people, went on three dates and none of them made me feel miserable for being sensitive. They made me feel valued, heard, and bothered. But I couldn't fix myself till then. I was scattered into pieces and some of the missing bits were still dimming inside Adith. I am not used to an easy-going relationship. I love difficult men. More precisely, I celebrate the impossibility of male hormones of being empathetic towards feminine emotion. I enjoy the tiniest amount of pleasure that comes after a skyful of pain. I am typical, rare and obnoxious, and I do feel pity for the people who aren't me.

One Saturday evening, Adith called suddenly and pulled me out of the house and took me to his hotel where he was staying for a week. After six months of disappearance, he just showed up from nowhere and dragged me into his den as I didn't possess a different entity in this world. He always had some invisible tenures that circled me around like standing in a piece of deserted island guarded in a deep, dark, mysterious ocean. There's no way to escape; there's no will to escape.

Reaching his place, the first thing he did was to pull out the lubricant from the drawer. It was a sealed bottle, and with just one tug of his teeth, the plastic cover got ripped off to the end. Placing the bottle on the side stand, his manly hands pushed me to the bed grabbing me by the waist. Eyes closed, slow and loud breathes, teeths clutter and lips met the crossroads. Adith's left hand was supporting me from the back and the right one was going upwards through my clothes and it stopped where it was supposed to stop. The never-ending manly desires towards the female bodies especially where it sensifies the most, was as true as a day. His hands always seek the comfort and softness of my breasts, and the very moment of making him hard and weak, turns me on. I love seeing men vulnerable. The ultimate patriarchy was just one blow away to beg redemption at my feet.

Now, I decided to take charge. I pushed him back and leaned him down to the bed pressing by his chest. I was on top, my legs opened over his crossed fold from where I easily pulled the chain and threw away his pants over the couch. He got up and leaned against the side pillow. Lights dimmed, sincere, whistly breeze and the slow scenes of me unwrapping my own body. I wanted him to see me naked, feel my skin, the scares, the pores, the stretch marks – feel it all. I wanted him to touch me, gulf me as a whole, but only after I let him be in me.

Two bodies, naked, warm and deep- dying to build home in each other. His ocean eyes were dizzy and flickering like Altair rhythming, the way I was riding him. He was trying to touch me, finger me in every way possible, but I didn't allow them to come along. The moment his fingertips awakened my senses through the scratches, I roped them for the rest of the night. The diabolic pleasure of seeing him drowning into sensation with his hands tied, voice choked and his soft moaning towards losing control with every second passed by, was unearthly. That was my night. The night of taking charge. I was the annihilation, the broken rule of my own tragedy.

"You aren't you today. Who are you in real?" – His voice broke in verse as I made him falter down frequently.

"Today, I am you, even more you than you can ever be."

"I don't want you to be me. It's dangerous and painful."

"Why do you care?"

"Why don't I?"

"Why would you? I'm just your side chick. More like a sex toy. Unless your hormones drive you crazy, you hardly remember my name!"

"You really think so?"- He scoffed.

"I believe so, with realistic proofs."

He lowered his eyes, placed his hands on my bare waist and smothered them all along my waistline to my throat. A gentle press, and he brought my face in a contagious distance and said, "Do you think I am good with this hide and seek? Do you think you are the only one suffering? You think I enjoy being off all the time?"- With his quirky words, his male organ was also getting harder. I felt it though my vagina, along with the warmth of his naked body.

"Prove it. Prove you are in pain, as much as you have given me. Show me your agony. Say you remember me on those happiest days of your formation as well as the hardest days of survival. Tell me the love song that reminded you of me, before you put it on repeat. Say, you look for me in every face you meet. Say it."- The eyes met and I poured all the seduction in my voice.

He kept quiet for long. Just a heave of sigh, defeating pain in his eyes, squeezed once, and a gentle bite, in his lips. The far I saw was an endless battle going inside. And he was fighting alone.

When my fingers touched his face, running down to his chin awakening sensations from the forehead, he seemed to be alive again.

"Ain't you gonna say how hopelessly you love me and........"- His voice was getting lower.

"Probably, I am gonna say something more!"

"I love you?"

"I desire you."- I whispered, touching his earlobes with my teeth.

That night, I didn't stop until he begged me with an embarrassing surrender in his eyes. I went off from his hold, dressed myself as before and put the lubricant into the dustbin. We produced enough moisture, seeping from every gland of our body, so a lubricant stood luxury to it. He was lost, shoring with the frigid wind coming through the wavering curtains, until I cupped his face and kissed him bye while closing the door on my way out. He didn't come down to watch me leaving, neither did I want him to. This way I made myself free from all the lust, desires and impure attraction towards him. I can love him from a distance, I can spend days drawing his picture in my head, but the volcano of sweltering needs inside my body, calls off his name and can stand the nights without the harmful urges of touching him. This was the day I treated myself with the utmost satisfaction to be calm, rigid and free from him. Body doesn't understand emotions all the time, but it does know where to, and when to stop. It was over, for me, for him. Probably in a way, none of us had seen it coming. I was tired of getting played, strangled and torn into pieces. And at this point of life, I solemnly understood that the more I would try to make him stay, convince him to lend me a place in his heart, the more he was gonna slip away. So, in any way or other, I had to unlove him. Doesn't matter if it would take a lifetime or two. A new life, new mind, a thick skin and bringing the pieces of the puzzle together, not holding onto things, but putting all down at my feet and seeing it getting dissolved in indecisive winds.

Summer came to my city again, burning, boiling, and melting down people's bodies as well as their fleeting desires. From our last encounter, four months had passed, and there was no sign of connection from any end. For me, it was a closed loop. I ended it after parting away the last piece of heart I had in me. For him, it was probably a break, maybe it wasn't anything, and this time I chose not to look for answers into his restless eyes.

In those months of surviving, Kanishk came home as he finished his summer internship early. Mom took us to aunt's house in Delhi to spend one or two weeks there, and dad joined us after two days. Unfortunately, and oddly, we met Ishaan there and mom invited him to have lunch with us. There he opened up about some serious family issues which I felt as the most irrelevant and severely disgusting to bring it onto the table. Even when I survived his boring conversations, he asked me out for a movie. It wasn't like a date; he was asking me to accompany him to the movie as an old friend. I would have said 'no', but my mom answered with an affirmation on behalf of me. So, I couldn't find enough space and courage to fit in a negation.

I probably did not remember Ishaan in these past few years of my utterly unnamed romance with Adith, but I could hardly forget each and every word he threw at me with the utmost annoyance, and negligence in his tone that ripped off my heart. Whenever I looked at his face, I saw a liar, a bastard who kept playing with my adolescent teenage feelings rather than stopping me where it actually ended. So, summing up with him again for whatever reason he gave, wasn't easy. Even while eating, I was looking at his face to find a new guy with responsible and plausible promises. In these few years, age had hardened him a lot. His frequently trimmed and strongly rooted beard, under-eye wrinkles, the uncared comedones - were signifying an obvious change in his presence. He smiled a little and asked if I wanted to go, and I slowly tilted my head to mom - like whatever she would say I was gonna follow her. I told Kanishk everything that happened between Ishaan and I, So at night, he also seemed convinced enough to let me go without any hesitation.

Next day, Ishaan took me up from my house and the trip-talk was mainly focused on how sorry he was for dumping me with some hurtful sentences that made me question my own entity. I was listening gravely and sometimes shaking my head for confirmation. In all these years of burning and suffering alone, he was nothing but a distant haze to me. He no longer mattered at all. His presence was unwanted and truly unrecognizable. He was no longer the guy I wanted in my life to walk through the black sands together. His presence was weighing me down rather than making me feel protected. But we reached the hall in a short time and now he had to stop blabbering.

The hall was one of the most luxurious movie halls in Asia, and after seeing the price of the tickets, my calculative mind actually started counting the fear of not being able to leave it midway. I went to the hall pretty quietly and took the seat for a reliving three hours of entering into a different world. Movies are meant to take you to a fascinating world, making you hope for a better life that these freaky directors are trying to show, but after it ends, you are still in the same crap you were before. At least, it fetched me a break from his forceful fake conversations, so I wasn't irritated that much.

The movie started at 6 in the evening with a hall packed with a preppy audience. The intimacy in those lovers' eyes, the overwhelming energy through the specs, the mysterious awkwardness of the first date and moreover the joy of coming with family - everything was there. People and their bright eyes were indicative enough to know that the movie was going to get a big hit. Ishaan was pushing back on his seat comfortably, palm supporting his jaw, engulfing the scenes playing in front.

It was probably 15 minutes before the interval when I heard the loudest noise that my auditory neurons can ever come across which even made the floor mats shiver. It was like bursting billions of firecrackers together maintaining the same frequency like concert pop songs within the teeming crowd. Some people were as confused as I was after being puzzled for some moments, and some people didn't even realize that it wasn't a part of the movie. I looked at Ishaan and he looked pretty unapproachable and unbothered about the surroundings.

I waited a few minutes to look at other people who were trying to figure out the source of the ear-wrecking sound and ended up getting nothing until the source itself came in front. I saw two rear exits banged open and a large ball of fire accompanied with smoke, weighing down the environment. Things got clearer when I saw scattered human body parts piling up into those fire and soon it got accompanied with undefined rounds of bullets. The shrieks got assorted with blood, sweat and the strong smell of burning flesh. Then, it took me sometime to realize that we were under a terror attack, like Paris saw in 2015, probably the attack, not even the meanest demons would like to see.

After few seconds, we were finally able to see the four figures, dressed in death, wrapped all in black, except the eyes and nose. They were made up with two rifles each and some of them even had more weapons.

"Ishaan, we are going to be dead in seconds."- My voice got choked, filled with the upcoming nasty figure of death. It got more prominent when one of the gun-points was at me and I couldn't help but look at the slowly visible figure of one attacker amidst the hue and cry. The moment I looked at Ishaan for help, I found him busy making an escape route for himself, and within seconds he vanished in thin air. It was me who just chose to sit and count moments to breathe before leaving the last one. My strength and willingness to stand out and run left me unguarded. My legs were trembling faster and my teeth were clattering to join the outrun. Standing at those final moments of life, I got a quick flashback of all the good things I extracted from the earth - like my mom, dad, Kanishk, Nikhil and even the shortest kindness I received from anyone I ever met. Like the way my neighbor never complained about my loud stereo, like the way the stranger in the metro supported my trolley so that it didn't slide through while I was sleeping, like the way the store owner downstairs always saved the last few chocolates and waited for me to come back from college, and a lot more. Kindness is free, it comes in so many forms. Sometimes you see it, sometimes you realise it through your own glasses.

My dreams were fluid, as factual as my realization. I deeply felt the slow death I dug for myself every day. Nobody was ever so cruel to me as I was to myself. I kept seeking validation from others, acceptance from the world, while hating my existence every single day with utmost disrespect. I tortured myself in such a painful way that no number of bullets can ever be able to cause me. The person I was running away from, was me, not any of these terrorists. *So, what am I actually scared of? Death? Ain't I dead already? They are just here to carry off my physical parts which were left to get burnt in fear of the society.*

Every day, I prayed to be dead, and when it actually came to me, I was scared and dull. My face was pale, my blood was ice cold, I was heaving like the normal breathers were falling short to fulfil my hunger. I was hungry to be alive again, to be loved again, to dance in the rain and smell the petrichor. At the gunpoint, I was actually convinced to love myself again with all the flaws, insecurity, ignorance, hatred and pity. A love that felt so right. A love - so very precious.

My life was at its end where I closed my eyes and saw my Adith's face with a whole-hearted smile. I wish I could see his face before I was gone forever. I wish I could touch him and feel his breath on my bare chest. But life is not about getting all the things you want; it's about appreciating the voids with the essence of living it. He was my desire from the rear to the front, from dusk till dawn. A life with him and a death wrapping up with his memories- Ah! How gifted I was with this life. *Thank you, universe. Thank you for everything.*

But the universe wrote some other destination for me which was written in a blood bath. When I opened my eyes, realizing I wasn't dead, not even hurt or scratched a little bit, I saw a familiar face in one of the black attires, dampened in blood and small pieces of human flesh, with an AK 47 slinging from his shoulder. Those eyes! Oh god! Those intimidating eyes, to stoop me to death.

It was Adith, but I can't assure if he was the same guy who used to plan a dreamy future with me. His calm and cold stares were enough to petrify me for life, while waiting for him to shoot me and fulfil his job. He came closer but he didn't shoot. His finger was not in the trigger when his eyes were confirming my presence in his real world. He wasn't looking at me - he was looking into me, again. The guy who made me crazy in love, the same guy dragged me to death that day. There was no shame, no fear, no regret, and now I knew where his luxury living came from.

He came closer and shot the camera fixed over my seat. The jimmying of the remaining, fell like some pixie dust smelling like death. He soon clutched my hand and scratched my body over the floor until the entrance hall came. What he did then, was an epiphany of time and memories which still keeps playing with me in a regular way. He grabbed me by my elbows and made me stand with those staggering feet, and pushed me towards the door and shouted, "Run" from a distance where his breath fell into my shoulder. This was the first time he spoke a word rather than communicating with those eyes where I saw love and death in different worlds.

All this time, my tears were silent and my strength was on rest, probably waiting for the ultimate nudge I was missing out. His words filled the magic in me that restored my strength to go out and run in real. That day, I ran. I ran for life. I ran to keep his word. I ran to run from the terror he was bringing on my table. And most accurately, I ran to save myself, to see a tomorrow again, to see the smile on my mom's face like I see whenever I am home. I wasn't done with life. I wasn't finished living, I needed it more, I needed more breaths to inhale, more paths to walk in and more flowers to smell - that more, the way it could fulfil me to the brim. So, I ran until I came out of the hall where the ambulances, police vans, normal cars, and the military forces were surrounding like a hawk.

I came out running and crushed to the floor like my legs were done carrying me. I didn't know whom to call, where to look and whom to trust. After a few moments, a nurse wrapped me up with a moist towel and took me towards the ambulance. I was shivering in fear and trying to swallow more air as it felt like the last straw of hope. I wasn't hurt a bit, but my clothes were drowning with the spilled blood from the dead surroundings. My wrist was still carrying Adith's fingerprint all around, as soon as the air drying process was fast. The nurse was trying to comfort me as much as she could, but she didn't know what I saw there. The brutal, naked reality of love where the conclusion was shimmering with death.

The militaries went inside and the whole galaxy cracked into pieces with those breath-taking fires. Both sides were fighting for lives, and soon the utmost silence engulfed the howling tears too. The military came outside and the hospital staff ran inwards. Standing at that moment, I didn't know if I should hate him for what he had done to humanity or should I keep loving the one who dreamt a new life with me.

Soon, my brother came and he found my face from his car window. He rushed towards me and with no time, the stiffness of his arms squeezed my breath. His hug was so tight that within a few seconds, he almost suffocated me. But that day he cried for me, at the verge of the feeling, where he thought he lost me for life. Everyone was shouting, messing around to see their loved ones, even for the last time. There were a lot of trays covered with white kaffan and all the sleepy, red faces were resting in peace. I saw a guy, looking for someone, flipping every sheet and still kept looking. In his flips, I saw some of the faces of terror who cloaked to death to stop firing. I looked for Adith's face in there, but I couldn't find any. One of the terrorists' bodies was in a visible distance and I went nearer to see his face with the anatomy. There was no doubt that he was one of the most authentic and pure beauties I had ever seen and he was even more handsome when calm and dead. Seeing him, The only thing that came to my mind was his mother. The poor woman would probably be in some corner of the world and praying for his well-being where he himself was snatching others' lives and parting other sons from their mothers. Adith was one of them too, and at that moment my body was too tired to look for him. So, I came back to my brother and stoned myself down in his lap.

I wanted to cry that loudest where the thunders would have hesitated to hear me out; but I couldn't. I wanted to run to Adith and demand him the reason why he had destroyed my whole life knowing that he would never change himself. Why would he spare me knowing that I am the only living proof of his rotten hands? *Why didn't you put the same bullet in my head too, Adith? Why did you abandon me again unlike you promised the last time?*

All my nerves were wrecking and twisting towards my brain till I could live no more. I thought I was dead until my eyes fled open again and I saw the sunshine from a small window of a hospital. I didn't have any idea about how and why I was there, laying, and pushing saline water in my body, but as soon as my body came into complete senses, I realized none of those were unreasonable. My body was on a strike with chronic anemia, low blood pressure and severe dehydration that got clubbed with mental trauma, and when I came back to life, I wasn't sure if it was any less painful to be dead. I wasn't in sense for almost 52 hours and all this time, Kanishk was there, sitting beside me, and banishing death with his care and prayer. Mom's tears were reckless, so the doctors suggested her not to enter into my room so frequently. Dad was busy managing her, where Kanishk was fulfilling the brotherly responsibilities for the first time in his life.

"Hey, you up all night?"- I asked Kanishk with a feeble tune.

"How's that information beneficial to you? Thank God, you are in sense, now you can swallow the tablets. I am tired of putting those under your tongue and checking it every 2 minutes."

"Thank you, Kanishk! I am grateful"- Those words came from the heart and I knew his hard outer shell had already started melting down.

He didn't say anything in return. He just looked at me sharply and flared a soft smile.

"Kenny, some gentlemen will come to meet you tomorrow. Be prepared for some questions."

"Questions? What questions?"

"Kenny, you know what you did, and it's just a matter of time for the world to know."

Suddenly, my throat stirred closed in dehydration. I looked at him and he seemed as difficult as he does, always.

Though I couldn't push a single word from Kanishk, I started believing my instincts when all my fear came true, strangling my breaths.

In the evening, after my soup, two gentlemen came and sat across, sticking their chairs with my bedsheet. Everything was too saner than it was supposed to be. The flapping sound of the plastic strips, pushing against the medicine tray, the deep and continuous hamming of the fan, and sometimes Kanishk's heel claps were perfectly audible.

Both the gentlemen looked at me very softly and showed their FBI badge before shooting their questions. I got to know that my boyfriend was no longer a secret, and the interests had been transmitted to the FBI as he was declared as a national threat. Among all the terrorists, Adith was the only one who escaped alive and despite those tight security checks, red alert areas, 'wanted' posters, and his face all over social media - it seemed like he vanished in thin air. Therefore, somehow, they traced me as his confidential affair and most probably the strongest living proof, so I was under trial, also as a national threat.

Though they kept my identity in veil after Kanishk made our lawyer talk to them, my whole extended family got to know I was in a romantic relationship with a terrorist. My dad was upset at first but things got cooler with time as my safety started bothering him much more than the identity of my boyfriend, and mom was surprised to see that I was in a relationship at all. It was a terrible thing to digest from someone like me, who hardly went through any romanticism in life, and when it happened, it happened ripping the world apart and taking some innocent lives. But my parents were more worried than shocked about the aftermath of the incident and now what kind of consequences I had to face just to prove I was also in as dark as others about his shady life.

They started with, "We will take very little time from you, mam, and I hope you know what this is all about."

I looked at Kanishk's face. He was perforating my eyes unless I raised a question in his. He then turned his face and started looking down like the way he does when he tries to strongly avoid my eyes.

I shifted my stare and nodded towards those gentlemen.

They started.

"How long have you known Junaid?"

I was startled and said, "Junaid?"

"That's correct. He faked his identity as Adithya, but according to our data, he's a guy with enormous identities. From them, we extracted that his real name was Junaid Isak Anwar, born and raised in a very small village in Madhya Pradesh, and got kidnapped and been sent to Afghanistan to train as a terror."

I lost my words as soon as the reality hit me. He lied to me. He lied about his identity. He lied about his life and probably everything we had. The person I thought I knew the most, suddenly he was someone I didn't know at all. He was a forger, murderer, a liar and a national threat to humanity. A sudden vision of his belongings flashed in front of me. The small negligible initials- J.I.A- which I never found to fit in a reasonable box. It was his name. His real identity. His luxury lifestyle, the bloody BMW, villa in Bangalore - everything came from the blood money. And I myself reaped the benefits of those, no matter even if it was for a day or for a year. So, now I can't just let it go for the sake of letting it go, because it wasn't only him. It was me as well, the very much of me who didn't even know what she was getting into.

He was not my Adith or Mr. Sen's absolute priceless Adithya. He was a terrorist. He was Junaid - a criminal who should be hanged or electrified for maiming the human race.

But even standing at that point, my mind was still not ready to detach him all the way. As I started drowning into my judgemental parameters, some part of my heart weighed more than my hatred. Probably he didn't lie, he chose to hide himself. He always talked about something he couldn't talk about. And I was the one who didn't listen. Probably I was scared of today that it might come someday; maybe not by endangering humanity, but probably in a less brutal way. Even though the roars and tears were still echoing from the walls, in my mind, I could only imagine myself standing at the highest cliff, withholding a life that had been dedicated to love him no matter what. *What's wrong with me! Why does it hurt so much, even after all the things he did to me? How did I fall in love with a terrorist? And after knowing all, why is it so hard to unlove him?*

"I don't know."- I finally spoke as I was seeing their patience was exhausting to bear with my silence.

"Mam, I want you to think. Think deeply about the time you were with him. He told you any of his work, where he lives, where we can find him, any address, email, phone. Anything? We went after his landlord as well, but that's not an option anymore."- one of the officers said.

"What? Why?"

"He passed away last month. As per data, he had a heart attack. They couldn't make it up to him."

My heart froze for some moments. Mr. Sen was dead as well as every good I had with Adith. He took away the happiness and all the parts that left came from pain, illness and suffering. But I was happy that he didn't need to witness this brutal outcome of his son.

Probably he wouldn't make it till today after seeing his Adithya's face all over the news channel. Wherever he was, I believe he was resting in love and peace.

"Do you have any information to offer us?" - He started again.

"No."- I didn't even look into them while saying this.

"Do you know you can also end up getting the same charges against you just because you aren't helping us at all!"

"No, you can't, officer. I was his victim too. The trigger was at me. I wasn't the one with guns."- At this moment, I scrounged my calmness from Kanishk's genes.

"But you are helping him to be alive."

"I am not helping anyone. Even if I would help, I wouldn't be getting anything in return. He was not a guy who would let you know a lot about him. He is still a mystery as he was before. He is still Adithya for me, I just heard about Junaid a few seconds ago. Seems like you already have more information that I could even offer you. So, don't push your words in my mouth. I said I don't know. He doesn't keep any connection with me. Neither did I try. So, you are welcome to speculate. I am so tired of all these things."

"You are pretty desperate as him. Don't you! No wonder, why you put up with him for so long! You are not an easy game at all, Ma'am. But I want you to know, these words can weigh you down to many allegations in court."- The first officer's tone had a firm warning.

"For fuck's sake, Kenny. If you know anything, spit it out. This isn't your home. They have had enough of your shit."- Kanishk howled out of nowhere. I was watching him tearing up all his gears to tolerate my adamant, and finally using his pitch to pull an end of this questionnaire.

I would've made him stop by words, but I could see no way to use those in front of a bunch of outsiders. Kanishk's outrage was not unreasonable.

I kept quiet.

The first officer again started," But we have ways to keep you out of this case. In case you are willing to help us with something."

I looked up into his face.

"We want you to make a phone call. Not today. Tomorrow. It's just a probable one. To reach him. We are suspecting that he's with this guy. And he will pick up the phone only when he knows it's you. You are the joker card here. And if you are denying for help, we have no option to skip your jail time." - He smiled without any hesitation.

"Are you threatening me, officer?"

"She will do it."- Kanishk pulled me up from the shore before I said something more nonsense.

"Okay then, mam, we are keeping your brother's word as a yes. He's an intelligent brat. You have to come with us tomorrow, early morning. Have a good day."

Both the officers stormed out with a filthy clacking of boots that started haunting the silence like my fruitless nights. I knew Kanishk was pissed, even I was pissed at myself for not being able to find where to start. I knew it was gonna get me through a long way from where there's no coming back. I had done something that was worth collecting a whole generation's hatred altogether, and still, I wasn't trying to get out of it. The officer was right. I was still trying to save Adith; not for him; but for me. I left some parts of my soul inside his subsistence. So, with him being dead, I am dead as well.

The next day, I was being driven back to a deserted place with my eyes blindfolded. But they didn't know that the roadmaps were sensitive inside my olfactory senses too, so, I could smell the places I passed by and some of them were absolutely undoubtable to me.

When we reached, it was midday already and I could only hear some thirsty crows on the roof. It was a one-storey building which was similar to the places where the kidnappers in Indian movies chose to keep their victims with minimum sources of living. The first thing they did was to rope my feet like I was trying to flee anyway. And later they brought me in front of a table which mostly looked like a mainframe computer with an attached receiver in it.

"Mam, have you got an idea already what you might have to do?"- In the history of English literature, I never found such a pathetic use of *'might'* at a wrong place and time.

"You have to make a call to your terrorist boyfriend and ask him all the questions clearly written in the script and buy us some time to reach him. You do it successfully, your identity will be a secret and your whole life will be saved. You can forget the whole incident as a nightmare. Else, we won't think a second to disclose your identity to the media where you should get ready to be hated for the rest of your life. This has become the greatest news in world terror also, so be ready to be on the front page of each and every newspaper in the world, and screw up your whole life including your family. You know different media will add different spice levels to your story. So, make smart choices."- The officer said it in such a cold tone, that I didn't even feel the need to suppress my decisions with some horrifying realizations. They left me with no choice. It was my family or me. And I had to choose them over Adith even after knowing that I would be the scariest criminal to them for the rest of my life.

I ran my eyes through the script, and it was clustered with some questions I knew Adith would never answer. But somehow all doors were closed in front and behind, so either way I had only one choice.

"Mam, are you ready?"- From that day, 'Mam' has become such an insulting word that I could never replenish it with some positive energy. I was dying a slow death and getting born again in a body with no me inside. The rest of my life was going to be a curse and I was not even ready to turn the steering in the reverse gear.

I nodded, and within seconds, one of the eleven officers pushed my skull with the nozzle of his gun. I was at the gunpoint for the second time in my life, and this time, it was actually more horrifying than the real terror attack as the button pusher would have nothing but utmost satisfaction if I were dead.

I picked up the phone and dialled the number. The giant screen in front of me started navigating but it was a complete failure as there were no receivers on the other end.

We tried once again but it was a dead end. The officer with the gun slammed it across the door and some "Damn it" slipped out from his mouth.

There was a grave silence in the roomful of twelve adults and suddenly I started feeling very unsafe being the threat to their male ego. I was shrinking in the idea of picturing my whole life as a grounded, unwanted and the most hated existence in my generation and spending it attending all the court dates and liquidating my dad's savings just because I fell in love with a terrorist.

After almost 6 minutes, one of the officers opened up, "What now?"

I didn't know if it was a magical charm or not, but the phone started ringing like a huge bang against the wall.

The officer again put his finger on the trigger and said, "Pick up the phone"

I looked at him once, and felt the nozzle in my forehead to finally pick it up.

WORDS OF THE DEVIL

I was the first one to say 'Hello', where I felt I gave the other person a little comfort with my female voice to say it back.

"Who's this?"

"This is Kenny. Is Adith there? Do you know where he is?"- Even after finishing this line my tears broke their bridge. Adith's name itself was an emotion to me, though I know he wasn't Adith at all. He was some guy who held the gun, and I was unlucky enough to witness that at a wrong place and at the wrong time.

"You called in a wrong number, lady. I don't know any Adith."- But somehow, I heard a tapping sound from the receiver. And I couldn't hang up the phone unless I heard another sound, saying, "Kenny?"

I was in a position to balance both our lives until I could balance no more. His name pushed away from my throat, "Adith" accompanied with tears.

"Kenny, is that you? How did you get my number?"

The scene in the room was worth catching eyes. The big screen had a vibrant moving picture of the caller's location. One officer was grabbing his headphones tight, to put his ears into our conversation. The man with his gun nozzle in my forehead, grabbed it strong, so that one bullet would be enough to stop my heartbeat.

I looked at the screen and asked mercy to the lord, with my heart storming inside out. I had to sacrifice all my love for the sake of my family and for all the families who lost their loved ones to the poison, I helped sowing.

"Baby, are you okay?"

Standing at the nearest point to death, I clearly realized that anyone of us would be dead after I end this call and there was no time left to waste over hinting. He was everything that I kept inside my heart safe, and realizing that this was the last time I was hearing his voice, I puddled my temptations to the extremity.

"I am okay. How are you? Where are you? You know, I wanted to talk to you so bad. I have a lot of confessions to make. Kenny, Kenny….. do you hear me?"

"Adith, why you did what you did?"- I broke into tears.

"I will explain it all Kenny. I will tell you everything. I know you will listen, I know you will understand everything…. Will you, Kenny? Will you? Tell me."- Then I heard him sobbing over the phone. I got petrified for a few seconds to hear him crying in real. The man who came from the dust to turn down fresh lives, was in tears- the tears of realization, the tears of turpitude, or probably the tears to picture himself as cold as death. Adith was crying - probably for the first time in his life - to a woman, who had no choice but to nudge him towards death.

The big screen now had fixed the pointer at a place, which was showing the location of a new city. The transmissions are going here and there but in written orders. Not a single person was making even the slightest sound in the room.

After 2,3 seconds, a handwritten note came to my table with deep and visible ink reading, "Buy us time."

So, now I had time to talk my heart out before another set of bullets tamed him for the rest.

"Adith, you are alright?"- My tears knew no bounds but consecutively I was feeling the gun grip in my head was getting pushed towards it. The small click sounds of the trigger, to let me know, if any of the situations were palpable through my voice, it wouldn't be hesitant to seal my mouth forever.

"I am sorry, Kenny. I am so sorry. You know, I am a fugitive now. You weren't supposed to see me the way you did. But now…..I have nothing to hide because you already know what I have been hiding all these days. I wanted you to know everything but not that way. I can be shot down anytime, and before I go, I want you to know everything. You deserve to know everything. You are the only good thing I had in my life and look at me now, I am about to lose you again, forever. How pathetic I am!"- His voice was trembling, aroused with sobs, and hearing him drowning this deep, my heart started pounding to crunch all the remorse, grief and tears to bring me the taste of death. He was the only will left for me to be alive. Even after knowing the terror he brought to humanity, I wasn't ready to live in a world without his footsteps. The ghosts could follow him to the dark and I didn't know how could I restrain myself from being jealous if I wouldn't choose to die!

"I wish I could tell what you are to me. How desirable, how wanted, how valuable is your existence. How could I repay your God to give me a blessing like you, knowing my hands are filled with blood. Kenny, you remember the day I saw you first? I never thought I would end up being this crazy for someone. I remember each and every detail of the day, of you, your smile, your words, everything. All these days I just wanted to talk to you because you know I have very limited time here. It's just not a confession, it's like finding some missing pieces of puzzle that could build either a poem or a terror. I chose the terror; Kenny, and I was wondered to see the depth of your love without asking anything in return. What are you, Kenny? A magic? How you did all the sacrifices jabbing your heart again and again.

I have seen you emptying yourself and pouring all the good in me. I have seen you burning, to light up my world. When I was unwanted, discarded from the whole world, you weighed me in and wrapped with the love I never had. You took me to the world where I have seen poems, happiness and willingness to be alive - to be alive for thousand fucking years, to love you for making my pathetic life worth living. I don't know how you made me dream about us! I started sketching a life with you, to wake up beside you every day, to touch your face every morning, to inhale your breaths when it's weighing you down. I look for you even when you aren't there. I look at everyone, every face. Try to find your glance to live one more day slicking you in my eyes.

You know, my friends now have a hold of you. Trust me, I never talked about it, but they have seen you bathing in my eyes. You emanate lives. I never wanted to be alive this bad. I wanted a life for you, to build you in my way, to love you in the way that you can't ask for more.

I thought within a connection gap, I will get over you eventually, but your God has destined something else that I couldn't get back to life pretending I never cared, where my whole world was falling apart just to see you for once. Whenever I look into you, I find all the missing pieces of me inside, a part of me is already flickering into you, it will live as long as you will keep it alive. Those eyes, Kenny, those eyes! Yours are the most dangerous and intimidating pair of eyes I have ever seen. Ever since I looked at you, my will to become a human again started flourishing. It's insane to be in love. It's even crazier that you made me fall for. Every day I waited for you to call me, to hear your voice, to tell me you love me, to touch your neck and flee to a different universe; just the two of us. I wanted you to dissolve into me where all my madness starts looking sane. And there's no end to it. Kenny, believe me, I am hopelessly in love with you and if I had given a choice to live without your love or to die laying in your lap, I would happily choose death. Do you still love me, Kenny? Say you love me! You still love me, right?"

I closed my eyes, trying to forget all the things happening around me - the shunning trigger kissing my forehead, thousands of people out there trying to locate him through me, the slow and marling gun-clenching sounds all over the air, the notices, his face of terror in every social media, and my restless heart dying for his touch even after knowing how badly mistaken I was at every moment of his living. My eyes were dizzy, my breaths were dying, my wills were desperate - "I do, I love you. Even after all these things. I can't stop..........I can't fucking stop. I can't help but loving you every moment. I miss you, Adith. I miss you every day. I miss your touch; I hear your voice in my dreams. I miss me even more when my clothes smell like you. Tell me a single way to unlove you the way you did. I can't Adith……….. I can't. I am sorry. I am so sorry, Love."- My tears were loud, and I couldn't even try to stop them even when I felt the trigger was at a push.

"Kenny, please don't cry. Don't cry for someone like me. Every time you cry, it hurts my soul like nowhere. You are my strong girl, Kenny. You are so strong that I forgot you were suffering.

I never unloved you, Baby. And neither could I ever. I surrendered to you a long ago, happily, willingly, cluttering all my desires from life to your feet. If I were you, I would preserve me to the eternity as my only woman of love! Or I would turn you to literature so that you stay alive through ages, as a magic. You are like the only flower bloomed into the streets, muffled with heavy gunshots, bathed in blood, but still, the fragrance of you weighs more than the blood stinks. I am just a corrupted man, with jabbed crack windows, cuts, wounds and thuds of blasts. I am darkness, and curse - death running through my veins where you planted love under my skin. Probably you never saw the storms, but I believe you felt the window clacking.

You remember the day you wore the black dress, neither crossing the knee, nor above your collar bones. You were beautiful, magnificent, and an impeccable sign of beauty like a goddess created as an art. I know you will hate me if I call you the goddess of night. But where the lights are at a deficit, how come you blinded my eyes with your beauty? I always wondered why you never appreciated how beautiful you are, how magical you are! Else, a guy like me wouldn't have died every time I felt your presence in my life. Even after seeing you that day, I tried forbidding my hands to touch you. My hands are of sins, Kenny. You never deserved my touch. I ruined you in so many ways that I am still learning to compensate those through my next life.

I still dream about a whole rainy night with you with no dead eyes, judgements, rushing against the clock. A night where we can be free and real, to taste the words of each other's mind. I would appreciate if we prefer silence over fake promises, but it's always you I never wanna quit staring at, for the night, for every time I be lucky enough to have you in my arms, even in my reality.

I know I was never the guy you wanted me to be, but the love you planted in me, the fragrance of life in your skin, the taste of death on your lips, and mostly the waves in your heart surviving through every storm - are mine. I have never been this crazy for someone in this life. Oh God! Kenny, why did you come that day? Why? Why? Dying has never felt this difficult. It's no longer a redemption, I want to live for you."- His sobs were audible, and mine was louder than the rain outside. I had never felt this worthless in my life where I was pushing my heart to die to make a meaningless life worth living.

"I know this call is being tracked and your investigators would find me sooner than you can even imagine, because I am letting them come to me. I wanted this to happen. I want to die when you are there, beside me, chanting a love song, ensuring you love me like before. All the things I did in the past - now my hands are soaked in blood. Every piece of my ribs will start trembling in hatred if I touch you with those hands. You are there, I can hear your voice, now I can die peacefully."

"Adith, listen to me, Adith no……… Adith."

Adith kept on saying, "One fine evening, when your world be at peace, when you will stop hating the last existing particle that builds you every day, I will take you out for a coffee and some conversations without the fear of pressing the trigger at any random moment. We will see a rainbow, we will watch a movie, we will have your favourite pasta, we will paint a wall with your favourite graffiti, will try some new ice creams and will sit back at a quiet place for hours before coming back home. I will drop you safe at home, bid bye to your parents, and go back with your smile shining all over my face. Kenny, I will be the guy you want, with every prospect, with every parameter, with every breath that wants me to be a part of you. I will be as you want me to be. A different identity, a different human being, probably the kindest one and moreover a guy possessing the best woman of human race. Maybe not in this life, but I promise you to come back to you again and again, in different shapes, at different places, through different people just to let you know that you are my only woman I loved and wanted more than anything. I am leaving my whole heart here, beating inside you every day, and I will come to take it back along with you. You are my possession, Kenny. And I promise, I will never leave you for any plausible earthly consequences. Till the day, you will breathe, I will breathe through you. Every atom of my existence loved you in a way the ocean loves the sky. You are the certainty. You are the bonfire of a frozen, stormy night. You are my lifetime comfort. Even the monsoon comes to make you feel loved, the raindrops do fall for you, and Kenny, I am just a human. You know, in between the first sight and this last goodbye, there was love - so much love I loved indulging. And a madness which kept me awake every night. I never knew I was capable of loving someone this much until you came in. I know it's tough, but till then, will you wait for me?"

"Yes, I will, Adith, I will. And I want you to know, I never loved anyone the way I love you. I love you more than anything, Adith. I………."- I was broken in pieces as my tears knew no shame who was there, who wasn't, and how they would think seeing me crying so hopelessly. I cried in the fear of the upcoming reality I had to face which wouldn't take my tears as a consideration.

Therefore, I heard a smirk and then a huge gunshot in a difference of few seconds which stifled me in a way I could move no more.

The officer who was eavesdropping my call, couched up and started shouting," Holy fuck! No, Nooooooo, Noooo, No……."

"Suicide?"- The other officer asked.

"Most probably. They are still on the way."

It took not more than 7 minutes to reach there and found Adith's body crossed with the bullet and the remaining of his brain scattered in the whole room. The guy who picked up the call, fled. They found no trace of him. Only Adith couldn't go! Most appropriately, he didn't want to go. He just wanted to be heard, to be understood, and to be gone while leaving me alone in a world full of demons. He lived by dying. He escaped from the world forever. A part of me died that day but I never shredded tears cursing my youth. I was his strong girl. Now, my way was to cross the creaking streets in a desert where the music of a violin turns into a dirge. Life wasn't supposed to be aesthetically satisfying, but I was the chosen one to see the cruellest side possible, and the only option left was to live.

Four Years Later

The turning point of Kanishk's life is here and we can't be happier enough to see him building himself again after hitting the ground so many times, and losing him in the process. After completing his MBA, he was in investment banking for a year where again he started whining about the work pressure and toxic people around. But a month ago, his weightiest interview clicked off. From next month, he's joining as a former CFO of a banking start-up which strikes his yearly salary nearly 10.8 Crores in Indian rupees. He will be staying in different places, and for the best, he's not trying to settle down anywhere. I wonder what his IAS friends are doing now, who was the happiest on the result day not for their own achievements but for my brother's failure. I hope they are also happy now with their peanut salary while waiting for the minister's approval to justify their actions towards a damaged road they failed to repair in some unnamed places of some unnamed cities of the most deprived part of India. I wish God gives them enough strength to digest my brother's victory over their limitless jealousy in these growing years.

He's earning the amount in a month which his whole bunch of batchmates have failed to earn in a year, so it's no longer a way to draw a parameter where the scales touch the both end of extremity.

I have seen him suffering in existential crisis, insecurities for putting his heart and soul into something and getting nothing but failures where the other door was opened to switch into his best, which again proved that he was even more perfect than his stupid self-doubts.

I have seen him growing up, reaching the peaks, doing the absolute that will make the average person shiver for a bit, getting heartbroken, smashed into the ground and standing up again and again to be his best. So, I haven't doubted him for a single second that something better was waiting for him and in the end of this pain, the deserving crown will fit into his head. I can't be any happier to be there on his best day. After Nikhil, he is my best boy now, where even the deadliest rivalry comes at a peace.

Nikhil has a nice life after IIT. A good job, a good wife and an adorable dog - everything fulfills him. Yes, he got married at a young age as his girlfriend's family was in a hurry, and Nik's parents didn't have any point of obligation. They are happy with each other so, what more parents can ask for!

If the topic comes to the most controversial part of my life, Adith never happened again. That intensity, that summer never came; so did my willingness to look for someone else. Ishaan left my side that day proving me right against all my family who thought getting back with him would be a good option. I am so glad that he chose to flee on his own, else my hands would have been dirty with his blood.

Adith was definitely a turmoil but it echoed in almost every personality altogether. Even for once in my life, I wanted to be loved so bad that each and every of my existing particles would be saturated by the love I never had, the love that can't be overflown anymore - he made me that satisfied to the brim. Like the nocturnal dark loves his moon, like the ocean dies for the tide, like the winter morning mourns for the sun, there was always an Adith for me. I never knew his reality, I never wanted to know what changed his past. All I wanted him to be that guy, what he was when he was with me.

I definitely make a lot of mistakes, but he wasn't one of them. He said he would turn me into literature if he had enough time to breathe. So, I've completed his unfinished part. My life is now with lesser adventures. Going to the office, finishing work, applying for Ph.D, taking complaints from the employees and listening to their personal vendetta in the time of coming back home. *Oh Adith! Why couldn't you stay a little longer?*

Though a Ph.D is not my choice, my parents want me to go for more. So I couldn't find a better option to keep their mouth shut. Degrees are the easier ways to erase your unforgivable past to your Bengali parents, so, it wasn't something that I had enough options on. But the one thing I still do for me is to write. Adith wanted me to be a writer and I am not letting him lose hope on me. Writing is the only thing, through which I can make him breathe again. It's probably illegal to love a man like him, but for me, he was my difficult man, and to love him again was never one of my bad choices.

If I get another life of freedom, a life with rainbows and shadows, I will choose him again. To stay with me in all the universes, by all the faces I can ever come across, in every identity I can always turn into. I will wish him again! Even if he comes with greater difficulties, I won't hesitate to ask for more.

BIGFOOT PUBLICATIONS
Invite you to join us